BROKEN PROMISES

By Ruth Ann Willis

To Lisa —

Enjoy!

Ruth Ann Willis

ISBN - 13: 978-1979853361
ISBN - 10:1979853363

DEDICATION

To Ralph for technical help, encouragement and support.

CHAPTER I

"Flight 720 to London is now ready for check-in." Analee heard the announcement as she hurried down the concourse. She was on schedule but liked to be early, if possible. Today the traffic was slow, and there was an accident on the interstate as well. Her Dad had dropped her off with a warm hug and a hearty "Bon Voyage."

Analee stood in the check-in line, observing her fellow passengers. There were the usual student-types with backpacks and water bottles, the businessmen in suits or dressy sweaters, and the vacationers excitedly chatting to each other about the sightseeing to come and the latest exchange rate.

"May I see your ticket and passport, please?" The agent smiled as he took her envelope. Analee had been so absorbed in the people around her she didn't realize she was already at the head of the line.

The agent handed back her papers as he said, "You're in seat 1A, first class, Miss Webster. Have a good flight."

Analee thanked him, turned away and glanced around for a seat. She still had an hour before flight departure. She noticed an empty row of chairs across the concourse and made her way to them. As she put down her purse and carry-on bag, she sank gratefully into the chair beside them. She watched the other travelers with interest, but did not notice a young man watching her from a nearby seat. He was thinking that she was a very attractive woman who seemed distracted and shy.

Analee Webster was twenty-three years old, a graduate of

Indiana University, on her way to London to visit her college friend, Nora Neubury. They graduated together in 1990. Nora had studied music and was giving a recital at Queen Elizabeth Hall. She had invited Analee to come for the recital and to see some of England afterwards. Analee was delighted to accept and had used the graduation money from her father to fund the trip.

Isaac Webster wanted Analee to travel a bit before coming into the family business. Time enough for her to be tied down to the restaurant. *Henry's* was a very popular, local spot in Bloomington, Indiana. Analee planned to join the business officially after this trip. She had worked there since she was old enough to wipe tables and carry dishes. But, this was different. Now, she would be part of management with her father, with increasing responsibility.

The young man shifted in his seat and thought about moving closer to Analee. Since they were to be fellow passengers, he thought they might as well get acquainted. Gus was on his way to London on business, but he liked to talk to people around him, selecting the shy, interesting ones for his attention. He tended to ignore the brash tourists, focusing instead on people who wouldn't broadcast their personal business and travel itinerary for all to hear. Using this criteria, Gus had met men and women from all parts of the world, in all sorts of occupations. He considered this part of his education as always ongoing.

Gus stood slowly, watching Analee, as he ambled toward her. He was dressed casually in neatly pressed khakis, blue oxford cloth button down shirt, open at the neck, and navy blue blazer. His bulging briefcase was a clue to the purpose for his trip.

He selected a seat across from Analee and smiled at her as he sat down. "Looks like they are about ready to board our flight," he said, as Analee glanced at him.

"Yes, I think so," she answered.

"Are you in first class, too?" Gus asked. "If so, we can board any time. They'll be serving champagne, you know."

Analee was surprised that such an attractive man would single her out for a conversation. She usually watched this sort of thing go on around her.

"This is my first time to fly first class," she smiled. "I'm usually way in the back. It's nice to know what to expect in first class."

Gus was about to tell her more when the announcement was made to begin boarding. He stood and waited while Analee gathered her bags and coat, and they walked together toward the boarding gate.

"We may have a full flight," Gus observed, noting the crowd surging forward. "I'm glad we're in first. Not so many feet to stumble over." He smiled at Analee, showing his even, white teeth.

"My seat is 1C, up in the nose of this 747," he said lightly. "Where are you?"

Startled, Analee drew back a little, saying, "1A. We must be near each other."

"Yes, we are across the aisle. These are single seats, first row."

"Oh," she said faintly, "I didn't know."

* * * * *

"Welcome aboard!" greeted the flight attendant as she followed Gus and Analee to their seats. "May I hang your coats and serve you champagne?"

Gus replied for both of them. "OK with me – we hurried to be first to drink champagne."

The flight attendant returned with two small stemmed glasses of champagne. "There you are. I'll check back for refills."

Analee stashed her bag in the overhead bin and put her purse and book on the floor beside her seat. She sat in the spacious seat, marveling at the size, as compared to her usual coach seat. She picked up the champagne, sipping it slowly, and watched Gus settle in.

He deposited his briefcase beside his seat, took off his blazer and handed it to the flight attendant. The pillow and blanket in his seat were carefully arranged to his comfort and satisfaction. Analee had folded her blanket on the armrest and punched the pillow behind her back. Time enough to settle in for the long flight. She observed Gus's six-foot frame fold into his seat. She liked his looks: the blond crew cut, wide shoulders and ruddy complexion. She thought his eyes were blue but hadn't looked closely yet. Her shyness with strangers, especially attractive men, kept her from getting too close.

Gus was doing his share of observing too, glancing over the rim of his champagne glass. He found Analee intriguing and appreciated her shyness. He didn't like women who were aggressive and pushy.

Analee appeared to be intelligent. He liked her All-American looks. Brown, short, curly hair, warm brown eyes, and her fair complexion pleased him. He wondered idly why she was traveling alone to London and leaned over towards her seat.

"Are you visiting friends in London?" he asked.

Surprised, Analee stammered her reply. "Y-yes, my college friend."

"Male or female?" Gus looked amused.

"Female. She's giving a piano recital this week."

Just then, the flight attendant appeared with the champagne bottle and cheerfully poured Analee's glass full with more bubbly. Gus held out his glass and winked at Analee as he lifted his glass in a silent toast.

Analee raised her glass in reply and sipped slowly. She wasn't used to attention from strangers, especially good looking males. Her father said she should be more outgoing, but she found it difficult even as she consciously made an effort.

"Ladies and Gentlemen, we are about to get underway. Please fasten your seatbelts."

Analee sat up and checked her seat belt, finished her champagne, and waited eagerly for the flight to begin.

Gus noticed her excitement and wondered again about the timid, mysterious woman he perceived Analee to be. He thought she might be an easy conquest if they could get together in London. He fastened his seat belt and handed his glass to the flight attendant, thinking about his own reason for traveling.

* * * * *

August "Gus" Herman and his partner had established a computer firm three years earlier, and it had finally taken off and was growing rapidly. As a result, their expansion had brought in business from England. He was on his way to see Ms. Elspeth Sheffield of Corporate Suites. He had spoken to Ms. Sheffield by telephone and was impressed with her, the firm, and the business plan. He felt he could assist her in reaching her goal, anticipating a very interesting meeting.

The 747 rumbled down the runway and lifted gracefully into the air. Both Gus and Analee were glued to their windows, watching the airport scenes flash by, then the expanding view of the city as the big jet climbed into the sky. Too soon, the clouds obscured the view, and they both sat back in their seats.

Soon the flight attendants began serving cocktails and dinner. When the cabin lights were dimmed for the movie, Analee decided she was too sleepy to watch and arranged her pillow and blanket for a nap. As she closed her eyes and drifted off to sleep, she shivered a little with anticipation for the adventure ahead.

CHAPTER 2

The big jet glided to a smooth landing at Gatwick Airport. Analee began to feel nervous. What if Nora wasn't there to meet her? Oh, she had assured Analee she would be, but Nora sometimes lost herself in her music, and time was suspended. This had happened more than once during college years, causing understandable concern for Analee now.

Analee knew that she had to go through immigration and claim her bags before she would even see if Nora was there. She followed the well-placed signs down the concourse and was soon at the "Baggage Reclaim" area. She noticed the sign being different from the airports in the States. As the baggage began to come around on the moving belt, Analee felt a hand on her arm. She turned and found herself looking up into Gus's blue eyes. He was smiling at her and said, "I'm Gus Herman. I'll be staying at the Park Lane Hotel. Maybe we could have a drink together one evening. Here's my card."

Analee drew back a little. Her reaction was mixed – flattered and frightened. She tried to smile and seem friendly, but aloof. "I- I don't know. Nora, my friend, will have my time all planned."

Gus was not put off by her response. "Are you staying with your friend?"

"Yes, she has a small house in Hampstead," Analee replied, too quickly, she realized. She wasn't sure he needed to know so much about her. He had all but ignored her on the flight after the first few minutes, working out of his briefcase most of the time. Now he wanted to get friendly!

Gus sensed her reluctance and smiled as he said, "Well, if you have a free evening, leave a message at my hotel." He turned, picked up his bag, and walked toward the "Way Out" sign above "Nothing to Declare."

Analee sighed, spied her bags going past and hurried to lift them off the belt. She looked around for a porter. "None to be found!" she fumed. "Just my luck to turn off Gus when I need a strong arm." Shouldering her purse and carry-on, she lifted a bag in each hand and walked out to the waiting area where Nora should be.

* * * *

Nora Neubury was notoriously late for everything. Today, she had hoped, no, *planned* to be early, or at least on time to meet Analee's plane. But, a conference at Queen Elizabeth Hall had taken longer than expected: then roadworks and traffic to Gatwick had delayed her further. Now she searched the car park for a parking spot, finding one seemingly miles from the terminal.

Running, her blond hair flying behind her, her coat flapping around her long, stocking clad legs, she hurried into the building.

Analee had emerged into a sea of strange faces, all peering past her, looking for their special passenger. Anxiously, she searched for Nora's familiar face. Not there. Now what would she do?

A row of chairs nearby, partially occupied by drivers and chauffeurs, seemed a likely place to wait while she sorted things out. She made her way awkwardly, burdened by her heavy bags. One of the waiting drivers sprang up, "'Ere Miss, let me 'elp ya." Analee gratefully accepted his help with her bags and sank into a chair. "Thank you so much," she gasped. The man touched two fingers to his cap and took his seat.

Analee glanced around and took in the scene. Crowds surged back and forth, as passengers came around the barriers and were met by relatives, or friends, or tour leaders gathering their groups.

A commotion further down the concourse attracted Analee's attention. There, trotting prettily on her high heels came Nora, parting the crowds with her beauty and commanding presence. Analee stood, watching Nora approach. She didn't want to call out, hoping Nora would see her and slow down, keeping so many people from watching them. Analee wanted to fade into the crowd, not be center stage. It was not to be.

Nora spotted her and cried out, "Lee – there you are. I'm so happy to find you. Sorry to be tardy."

Everyone was watching, Analee thought. Nora reached her and hugged Analee warmly, kissing her on both cheeks. "How was your trip? Did you have a smooth flight? Are these your bags?" The questions came rapidly as Nora began gathering Analee's things.

"I hope you haven't been waiting long. My conference about the recital lasted longer than expected, and I couldn't get away." Nora chattered on as they made their way through the crowd to the car park.

* * * * *

Nora's small car was a delightful surprise to Analee. She had expected to take the train to Victoria Station. Nora had given Analee detailed information about Gatwick Airport and London while they were in college. Analee loved to hear her talk about England and all the attractions. Now, she was actually here.

"I can't believe I'm really here at last," she smiled.

Nora opened the "boot" to stow Analee's bags. She joked, "You ain't seen nothin' yet, Lee. Let's go!"

Nora threaded her way out of the parking area to the highway and sped along, past the green fields and charming stone farmhouses. Analee busily turned her head from side to side taking it all in.

"So, did you meet anyone interesting on the plane?"

Analee blushed a little. "Well, a man did talk to me."

Nora grinned. "Did you talk back?"

"A little, but he was busy working most of the time." Analee knew Nora wanted the details, but there weren't many to give. "His name is Gus Herman, and he's at the Park Lane Hotel."

"Wow!" Nora squealed. "You must have made an impression on him. Did he ask for your phone number?"

Analee sank further into her seat. "I told him I was staying with a friend. He asked me to call if I had a free evening," she mumbled.

Nora was happy to hear that Analee's shyness had not

completely baffled the man. During their college days, Analee had turned down dates because she was afraid she wouldn't know what to say. After several attempts at dates, encouraged by her friends, Analee was convinced she was a complete dud with men.

They arrived at Nora's pleasant little house and pulled to a stop in the short driveway. Analee looked around at the neighborhood, noticing the attractive houses lined up like white dominoes set on end. Each one had a small porch, clipped hedge, and front bay window. Lace curtains hung behind sparkling glass. Analee was enchanted.

CHAPTER 3

"Come on in" Nora chirped. "Let's get you settled and have some tea." She led Analee through the front door into a small entry, which opened into the dining room. On beyond was the living room with tall windows overlooking the garden. The furnishings were typically Nora – eclectic mix of fabrics and colors with paintings on the walls done by artist friends. Dominating the living room was Nora's grand piano.

"Don't mind the mess," she said as she swept music books off the piano bench. "I practice most of the time and never get around to straightening up."

Analee thought the room was charming and said as much.

Nora motioned her through a door at the end of a narrow hallway. The house had been remodeled before Nora purchased it, and the large front room was now Nora's bedroom. It contained a wide window seat across the front, piled high with padded cushions and antique dolls. On the side was a fireplace, fitted with a white, ornate mantle. A chaise lounge sat on a hooked rug. Analee thought it was a cozy hideaway. Nora smiled, "It is my refuge at the end of a busy day."

Nora moved back to the hall. "Your room is here."

Analee entered a small room at the other end of the hall. The room contained a single bed, covered with a white and blue comforter. A floppy, stuffed rabbit sat on the foot of the bed, and white lace pillows lay against the headboard. Tall windows above a window seat were covered with white vertical blinds, now open to the view of the garden.

"There's a bath over here," Nora pointed to the other side of the room, "and a closet. I think there's enough room for your things, but it might be crowded."

Analee was overwhelmed. She felt she was in heaven and pinched herself to be sure she wasn't dead.

"I'll leave you to unpack and freshen up while I make some tea – OK?" Nora breezed out of the room and closed the door. Analee flopped backward on the bed while she took in her surroundings. The wall behind the bed was covered with bookshelves, filled with intriguing books. She wanted to investigate each one, but knew she couldn't yet. Nora expected her to be ready for tea in a few minutes.

She rummaged in her purse for the luggage keys and opened her bags. Nora was right; there was barely enough space in her crowded closet for Analee's things.

She dug out a pair of slacks and a turtleneck sweater and took off her traveling suit. She felt grimy from the trip and decided she had time for a quick shower.

Analee hopped in the shower stall and felt the strain of the trip run down the drain with the warm, fragrant water. She hurriedly dried herself and dressed in her new clothes.

She had splurged on a new wardrobe for the trip. Her mother insisted she needed new things, since her college wardrobe consisted mostly of jeans and sweatshirts. Analee's mother had excellent taste, and they had gone shopping several times until the task was completed.

Now she looked at herself in the full length mirror on the closet door. "Mom was right," she thought to herself. "This outfit is very flattering."

As Analee stepped out of her room, Nora stuck her head out of a doorway. "Come on into the kitchen. Tea is just about ready."

Nora's kitchen was another marvel. It had all the usual appliances, with one wall of cabinets above a small counter. Across the room was a door to the outside, and Nora explained it opened to the space between houses.

Analee wandered into the kitchen examining everything. She wanted to remember this place. It was like a playhouse!

"What is this thing?" Analee pointed to a white, boxy-looking appliance next to the back door.

"It's my washing machine," Nora said, glancing over her shoulder. It washes and dries, too.'

"I've never heard of such a thing!" Analee exclaimed. "Does it take very long?"

"About an hour – very efficient. Are you ready for tea?"

Analee followed Nora to the dining room. A teapot was covered with a colorful tea cozy. Pretty china cups and saucers sat beside it. A plate of cookies was placed between them. They sat down, and Nora lifted the plate.

"Have a biscuit?"

Analee started to reach for a cookie, then drew back. "Biscuit? Where?"

Nora giggled. "We call these biscuits. Take one, go ahead."

Slightly embarrassed, Analee lifted a biscuit off the plate and bit into it.

Nora poured tea and added milk to hers. Analee nodded when Nora motioned the pitcher toward her cup. "I'll try it," she said softly. One sip of tea told her she had made a good decision. "It's delicious. Maybe I'll learn to be British!"

They chatted about Nora's house, college friends, Analee's job, and Nora's recital while they drank their tea.

Analee sighed contentedly and leaned back in her chair. "I feel refreshed. What's next?"

Nora got up and began to clear the tea things. "If you're up to it, we'll take a drive to Queen Elizabeth Hall, and I'll show you where my recital will take place."

"Oh yes, please." Analee's eyes shone with delight. "I want to see everything."

"All in good time," Nora called from the kitchen.

* * * * *

The two piled into Nora's car, and she sped off, negotiating the narrow streets with ease. Analee held her breath as they wound around, narrowly missing the oncoming cars. She hoped Nora knew where she was going.

"I am hopelessly lost, Nora. How do you ever learn your way

around?"

Nora grinned. "It's easy, love. Just follow your nose!"

They arrived at Queen Elizabeth Hall and Nora pulled into a parking space marked "Reserved." Analee gulped. "This is someone's private spot."

Again, Nora just grinned knowingly and said, "Follow me."

Analee wondered if the car would be there when they returned but bravely set out after Nora. They entered a door marked "Performers Only" and followed a narrow hallway. Suddenly, there it was! The cavernous auditorium called Queen Elizabeth Hall, beautiful, ornate, and historic.

Analee gasped and her eyes widened. She slowly turned around and around, fascinated, not wanting to miss any detail.

"Come on now." Nora was tugging at her arm. "I want to show you my practice room."

They finished their tour of the Hall and walked slowly out of the building. Nora's car *was* still there despite Analee's misgivings. She would have to learn to trust Nora.

"Tomorrow night there is a party at my agent's house. It should be fun, and you can meet my fellow musicians." Nora spoke rapidly and fiddled with the key as she put it in the ignition. Her hair swung across her face. Analee wondered if she was hiding something.

"Are you sure I should go?" Analee said softly. "I don't want to crash anyone's party."

Nora straightened. "Of course you should go. Don't be silly. They're expecting you." She backed quickly and eased into the traffic. "There's a lovely Italian restaurant near here. Shall we have an early dinner?"

Analee nodded her agreement. Jet lag was beginning to catch up. It would be good to get to bed early.

* * * * *

They arrived back at Nora's just in time to catch the telephone ringing. Breathlessly, Nora ran to answer it.

"Hello?" She said quickly, then smiled. Her voice changed to a low, soft pitch. "Yes, she's here. We just came in from having dinner." Analee crept softly to her room, not wanting to disturb

Nora's conversation. It sounded like a very personal call.

Analee took off her clothes and pulled on a soft, warm nightgown, over which she wrapped a matching robe in soft, pink cotton flannel. She pushed her feet into pink slippers and went into the bathroom to clean her face.

Nora knocked softly and opened the door. "Are you decent?" she called.

"I'm in here," Analee answered, "and yes, I'm decent. Come in."

"I want to talk to you," Nora said with a catch in her voice. "There are some things you should know." She plopped down on the bed and folded her legs under her.

Analee sat next to her, wiping the cold cream off her fingers with a tissue. "What things?"

"For one, I'm moving to Paris after my recital. There's a teacher who has agreed to accept me as a student. It's the Paris Conservatory, very prestigious. I need the training I can get there in order to further my career."

"That's wonderful!" Analee hugged her friend. "Really good news."

"There's more." Nora bent her head, causing her hair to swing across her face, hiding it. "I'm getting married – to my agent, Martin Giles." She stopped, holding her breath, waiting for Analee's reaction.

"That's wonderful, too!" Analee laughed and again hugged Nora. When's the wedding?"

"Tomorrow. The party I told you about is the reception."

Analee's eyes widened as she leaned back and looked at Nora. "And when do you leave for Paris?"

"Sunday."

Three days away. Analee's thoughts were jumbled, trying to absorb this turn of events. The recital was Saturday evening. What was to become of her plans to sightsee in England?

"Nora, how long have you known about this?"

"It happened so quickly, I didn't have time to tell you or change your plans. Anyway, I wanted you to come. Are you angry with me?"

"Nooo," Analee said uncertainly. "I'm really happy for you, Nora, and glad I can be here to see your wedding."

Nora brightened and stood up quickly. "I have a travel agent friend who is taking a group on a special English Castles Tour. She has agreed to add you to the group. I know you were looking forward to touring the British Isles. You will, just not with me."

Analee smiled at her friend. "Thanks for your consideration, but I don't think I would be comfortable on a group tour alone." Her usual shyness was back, front and center.

Nora's eyes narrowed. She stood up with her hands on her hips. She stared down at Analee. For a long moment, she said nothing. "Lee, if you ever want to succeed in life, in relationships, even with yourself, you have to let go and do things. You are a sweet, charming woman. Now, it's time to let the world see you." She spoke emphatically, punctuating her words with both hands, index fingers pointing.

"But Nora, I never know what to say to people," Analee whined softly.

"Just smile and listen," Nora instructed. "People love a good listener and you won't have to talk. Ask a question now and then, and they will go on and on."

Analee took a deep breath and blew it out. "I- I guess you're right," she said uncertainly. "When does the tour leave?"

"Sunday morning," Nora smiled. "You will meet Margaret at the party, but you will need to move to the Park Lane Hotel. The tour leaves from there." Analee felt as if her life was on fast forward. All the plans she expected were changing into something frighteningly strange. She felt out of control.

Nora leaned over and hugged Analee. "Let's get some sleep. Things will look brighter in the morning. Good night, sleep well." She backed out of the room and softly closed the door.

Analee still sat on the bed, stunned by the turn of events. Finally, she dragged herself up, dropped her robe on the foot of the bed, and climbed in between the cool sheets. The bedside lamp glowed warmly beneath the bookshelves. Analee was too devastated to even think about investigating the books. She lay there for a long time, her mind spinning with all the new developments. She was sure there would be no sleeping tonight but reached over to click off the lamp.

CHAPTER 4

The next thing she knew was the feeling of warmth on her face and opened her eyes to find sunshine coming through the windows. Nora was knocking softly.

"Are you awake? Breakfast in 15 minutes," she called cheerily.

Analee struggled free of the warm covers and shivered. She wanted to burrow back in the snuggly warmth, but instead, swung her feet over the side and into her pink slippers. Wrapping her robe around her, she wondered if Nora minded her appearing at breakfast in her robe. After a quick glance in the mirror and a finger comb of her hair, she stepped out of the bedroom to the smell of freshly brewed coffee.

"Well now, good morning Lee." Nora grinned as she carried a tray to the dining room. "I have coffee and muffins ready. Would you like eggs?"

"No, muffins will be fine." Analee smiled back. "Good morning to you."

"Sleep well?" Nora set a cup of coffee at Analee's place and motioned her to the chair.

"Surprisingly, yes I did." Analee blew on her steaming cup as she spoke. "Considering the shocking news and jet lag, I was expecting a sleepless night."

Nora smiled. "You're going to be fine. Margaret will take good care of you. I know you will like her." She jumped at the sound of the doorbell.

"That will be Martin, my fiancé. He said he would pop in this morning."

Analee panicked. "But, I'm not dressed! I can't meet anyone in my robe and with no makeup!"

Nora waved her hands. "Nonsense. Martin won't mind. He's seen girls in robes before."

She opened the door to a short, balding man with twinkling emerald green eyes that crinkled at the corners. Analee thought he was the happiest looking man she had ever seen. No wonder Nora was marrying him. Their life would be full of joy.

Martin rushed past Nora, giving her a quick peck on the cheek. He strode across the room to where Analee sat, too embarrassed to move.

"Hello, Analee. I've heard so much about you; I feel I know you already." He stuck out his hand, and Analee, responding to Martin's friendly gesture, lifted her hand to his. She felt it clasped in warmth, feelings of strength flowing into her. She forgot her appearance as she looked into his eyes, mesmerized by their depth.

"Y-You have the advantage," she stammered. "I only learned about you last night."

Martin's booming laugh filled the room. "Nora has been keeping me secret, has she?" He turned to Nora, putting an arm around her, still holding Lee's hand.

"I've come to take two beautiful ladies to lunch. Then we have a date with the vicar." He turned to Nora and squeezed her shoulders. "Are you ready, love?"

Analee wondered if Martin was Irish – he certainly seemed full of blarney.

As if he had read her mind, Martin said, "Did Nora tell you I'm half Irish? My mother came from Dublin as a girl, and she has been a big influence in my life." He grinned. "Just thought I would throw that in."

Nora turned to Martin giving him a little kiss. "Mr. Giles, you'd better let us get ready. I have to look like a bride."

"Darling, you are a bride. My bride, and your looks are perfect." Martin held her close for a moment and then gave her a little push. "Go on then, get ready. I'll be back in two hours. I need to get dressed like a bridegroom myself."

Martin leaned over to Analee, who still sat at the table, wide-eyed and pale faced. He planted a kiss on her forehead and ruffled her hair. "It's OK, Analee. Things will slow down soon." Giving her a warm look, he slowly turned and went to the door, opening and closing it softly.

It seemed to Analee that he just vanished into thin air. She shook her head and looked at Nora. "I can see why you love him. He's enchanting – and I've just met him. Is he always like that?"

Nora's eyes were glowing. "Yes, isn't it wonderful? Martin really swept me off my feet."

Both women rushed to their bedrooms wasting no time in the preparations. Martin inspired that feeling in them, and in everyone he met. As a result, they were both waiting when Martin returned.

He had changed into a beautifully cut, black pin striped suit, crisp white shirt, and red and black striped tie. His appearance was somber until one looked into his eyes. They sparkled with emerald green lights.

Nora's outfit was a creamy, white silk suit, embellished with pearls on the fitted jacket. The skirt was short making her shapely legs look longer. On her feet were high-heeled, white sandals and in her ears, antique pearl earrings.

Analee thought she had never seen a bride look so lovely. Her own dress was one she had thought would do for an evening out in London. It was royal blue, silk knit, with matching jacket. Around her neck, she wound a royal blue scarf which was woven with gold threads. Her earrings were gold hoops. She wore a gold and diamond bracelet on her wrist, a graduation gift from her aunt. Analee wondered if she was suitably dressed for a wedding.

Nora eyed her carefully. "Lee, you are stunning! Where have you been hiding?"

Analee felt more confident as she grinned at Nora. "College days didn't exactly demand dressing up," she joked, " but it feels right now."

Martin linked arms with both Analee and Nora. "You two are the most gorgeous females in London today. Let's go!"

* * * * *

The trio roared away from Nora's in Martin's little car with Analee hanging on to her seat belt in the back seat. They headed toward Piccadilly for lunch at the Ritz. As they drove up to the hotel, attendants rushed out to open the doors and assist the women. Martin tossed the keys to one of the attendants. "We'll be here about two hours. Park with care."

The women walked ahead into the lobby. A man and woman sitting on a bench stood up and sauntered toward Nora and Martin.

"Hello, you two," the woman called. "You're on time for once." Her delighted laugh rang out as she hugged Nora.

Analee stepped back uncertainly. Martin took her arm drawing her forward saying, "Lee, these are our friends, Elspeth Sheffield and Robert Warwick. Elspeth owns a firm called Corporate Suites, and Robert's bank handles our financial affairs."

Analee shook hands with both of them and felt herself being assessed by Elspeth, who was fashionably attired in a ruby red, wool dress. Simply cut, it clung to her figure in all the right places. She wore a dazzling ruby necklace and matching earrings. Her mink coat lay casually tossed on the bench behind her. Analee wanted to sink into the floor or turn and run, whichever she could do quickly. But then, Elspeth smiled, and her face changed from cold to warm, black eyes sparkling.

"Nora has told me about her friendship with you, Analee. Welcome to London."

Analee was so taken aback, she said nothing, arranging a pleasant look on her face.

Nora, watching the effect Elspeth had on Analee, hoped she would soon learn that Elspeth's success in business was due, in part, to her ability to assess people, much as she had just done with Analee. Elspeth's business contacts were usually put off by her cold, calculating look. The bold ones were impressed with her ability to analyze a situation and find solutions to problems.

Just then, Martin who had gone ahead to see about their table hurried over and said, "Let's go in to lunch. It's all ready for us."

Elspeth picked up a box from the bench. "Here are the flowers, Nora. I picked them up from the florist, as you asked. They are beautiful, I must say."

"The florist is a friend," Nora smiled. "I knew the flowers would be lovely."

Analee managed to get through lunch, actually rather enjoying the conversation going on around her. Elspeth, Robert, and Martin took turns regaling the group with stories and funny anecdotes. Analee remembered Nora's advice and tried to ask enough questions to keep the others talking. She found it rather easy to do, but then, these were sociable, outgoing people at ease with each other.

* * * * *

They were enjoying coffee when Nora glanced at her watch. "Martin, dear, we should be off to the vicar. He is expecting us at four."

Analee wondered if all of them were to go along for the ceremony. Elspeth stood and faced Nora. "My dear, I know I told you I would witness your wedding, but a business matter has to be dealt with today. My office in Spain has a crisis, and I must go now. Perhaps, Analee could stand up with you." Blowing a kiss to Nora, Elspeth breezed out of the dining room, trailing her mink over her shoulder.

Nora was stunned. She had counted on Elspeth and Robert to be their witnesses. Of course, she wanted Analee to be there, but now she would have to be the maid of honor.

Analee also was alarmed and frightened. Things were happening too fast. What was going on with these people?

Nora turned to Analee and hugged her. "I know you are feeling rushed, my friend. Can you 'come in from the wings and fill the role?'" Her eyes were filled with concern as she looked at her friend.

Analee loved Nora, her closest friend, and wanted to do whatever she could, but she was having a hard time keeping up! After a minute, she spoke, "Of course I will, Nora. It will be my pleasure to be your maid of honor." She took a deep breath. "I can handle it."

"Good girl!" Nora beamed her relief. She turned to Martin. "Darling, we should be going. Will you get the car?"

Martin had been watching the women with concern of his own and now responded to Nora's question with a quick nod.

Robert offered his arm to Nora. "Come, the vicar awaits." Analee followed them to the door where Martin's car had just been brought around.

The four rode in silence to the chapel where the wedding ceremony would take place. Each of them was having his own set of nerves. The vicar was standing on the steps of the chapel when they arrived. He was a large man, with white flowing hair. He greeted them with a smile, and they all went inside.

The ceremony was short but beautifully done. The vicar's words, spoken in his soft, compelling voice, recited the timeless vows. Nora and Martin, eyes on each other, responded with their "I do's" while Martin slid a gold band on Nora's finger. It was done.

Robert took Analee's elbow and guided her to the door. "I'll drive and you can sit in front with me. The lovebirds can sit in back."

Analee nodded her agreement. They walked down the stone steps of the chapel, Martin and Nora following.

CHAPTER 5

Martin's house sat in a fashionable London area called Belgra-via. From the outside, the building looked tall and imposing with high, narrow windows and doors. Across the front at the edge of the sidewalk, ran a row of stone pillars connected by pointed iron posts. Analee felt intimidated by the building and the party inside. She was not comfortable in a crowd of strangers, even if they were Nora's friends.

Cars were parked all around the square. Robert maneuvered the car into a small space. He opened Analee's door and offered a helping hand as she got out. Nora and Martin were still engrossed in each other in the back seat. They realized the destination had been reached and slid out of the car, still holding hands.

Robert grabbed Analee's hand and said, "Come on; we'll alert the party that the guests of honor are here." They stepped up to the tall double doors, and Robert swept them open.

"Attention my friends! The bride and groom have arrived."

The group of people turned as one. Expectant faces looked toward the door. Nora and Martin paused and acknowledged the burst of applause with a wave of their hands. They stepped into the crowd, accepting the hugs and handshakes of congratulations.

Robert spotted friends and ambled over to join them, leaving Analee alone just inside the door. She backed up to the wall, trembling slightly. Her knees felt ready to buckle. She thought she might be sick. "I must get away from here," she thought, as her gaze roamed, searching for a convenient escape. The party seemed to be concentrated in the living room on the left. A door on the right appeared to lead to a study or small library. Analee fled to this sanctuary, praying that no one noticed her.

Across the room Gus Herman had watched the entrance of the bridal couple. He didn't see Analee at first, but when she crept across the hall to the study, he made his way through the crowd to follow her. Gus understood how she might be feeling and thought a familiar face would be welcome.

He slowly opened the door to the small room and looked around for Analee. At first, he saw no one, but just then a slight movement caught his eye. Analee was huddled in the corner of a small settee, hands over her face with her shoulders shaking. Gus rushed to her side. Prying her hands away from her face, he looked at Analee with worried concern. "Are you OK? Has something gone wrong?"

Analee slowly raised her head, tears in her eyes. She was surprised to see Gus, but her feelings of helplessness overcame her surprise. "I have made a terrible mistake," she whispered. "I must leave here and go home."

Puzzled, Gus gripped her hands. "What kind of mistake?" he asked gently.

Analee sighed. "I thought I knew Nora so well. We were best friends. She invited me here for her recital and sightseeing. Now she's married and leaving for Paris. I'm not ready to be on my own in a strange country. It will be best if I go home."

Gus continued to hold her hands as they sat, each lost in thoughts. Gus's hands felt strong and warm to Analee, and she drew comfort from them. Gus said thoughtfully, "I have an idea. My business in London will be finished in a couple of days. I was considering staying on for some touring. I would like very much for you to join me." He turned to Analee, smiling gently. "What do you say?"

Analee was confused. Why was Gus taking an interest in her – Analee, the shy, timid nobody that people ignored? Was it possible that he really meant what he said, that he *liked* her?

Gus sat watching Analee, her face changing as the thoughts raced through her mind. He thought he knew what she was thinking and waited for her reply.

"I don't know what to say," she whispered at last. "You know nothing about me. I wouldn't be very good company. It's probably best if I just go home."

Gus wanted to hold her, to transfer some of his own confidence to Analee, but he knew it was too soon. She was such a shy, little bird! He spoke firmly, "Let me be the judge of your company. We can have a great time together. Please say yes!" He was still holding her hands, and he squeezed them again then let go. He had an idea about how this adventure would be advantageous for him.

Analee looked at him through still wet eyelashes. "May I let you know later? I need to speak to Nora. She had made some plans for me."

Gus nodded his head and stood up. "I'll be around for a couple of hours. Please give my offer serious thought." He stepped to the door, turned and grinned at Analee before moving on through to the hall.

Analee sat thinking. What should she do? Surely, Gus was trustworthy – she could sense his honesty and caring. She just wasn't accustomed to charming men. She must find Nora. What was it Nora had said? A tour leaving from the Park Lane Hotel?

Before she could move, the door swung open, and Nora's head appeared. "Lee, what are you doing in here? I've been searching the house for you!" She marched across the room to where Analee sat on the settee.

"Why, you've been crying. What's wrong? Are you ill?"

Analee sobbed out her confusion to Nora, ending with a soft wail, "I want to go home."

Nora was puzzled at Analee's behavior. She had been so willing to go along with Nora's plan to put her on Margaret's tour. Now, Analee was a sodden heap, anxious to return to America. Nora sat down and put her arm around Analee's shoulders. "Lee, are you letting me down after all my pep talks? Remember, I said it was time to let the world see you."

Analee sighed and hiccupped. A slight giggle escaped her lips. She was on the verge of hysteria. "I remember," she said softly. "There's another complication. Gus is here – the man I met on the plane – and he has suggested we tour together for a few days."

"But that's wonderful!" Nora declared. "The perfect solution." She wondered to herself how he was connected to her friends, and to be included in her wedding reception. She would check it out.

Analee sighed again. "I don't know. Gus seems to be sincere, and I do like him, but I barely know him. Do you think it's safe?"

Nora stood quickly. "Come on. Let's go fix your face, and we'll find out about this Gus."

A few minutes later, Nora and Analee reappeared and began making the rounds of the partying guests. After several discreet questions Nora was completely baffled. No one seemed to know Gus, or why he was here.

"I suppose we'll have to ask Gus himself, awkward as it may be," Nora mused.

Gus was leaning on the mantle, gazing into the fire blazing in the fireplace. He had been watching Nora and Analee and suspected their motive. He was not surprised when the two women approached him.

"Hello, I'm Nora Neubury, er...Giles now." She blushed as she remembered her newly acquired name. "Analee is my friend, and she tells me you met on the flight over."

Analee stepped back, but Gus reached out and drew her nearer. "Yes, we shared champagne and had adjacent seats in first class." Gus smiled down at Analee as he spoke. She felt his warm fingers on her arm. A surge of confidence ran through her body, and she smiled back.

Nora noticed Gus's effect on Analee and plunged on. "Do you know someone else here tonight?"

Gus heard the unspoken question. "I was invited by my business contact in London, Elspeth Sheffield. I don't think she's here yet."

Nora's eyes narrowed. "Elspeth invited you?" Nora's voice rose. "Then, she decided her business in Spain was more important. She's not coming."

Gus was surprised, both at Nora's vehemence, and by the news that Elspeth was not going to be at the party. She had assured him that he would meet valuable business contacts here, and she would introduce him.

"I'm sorry if I've crashed your party. Elspeth didn't tell me it was your wedding reception. But since I'm here, Analee needs a friend. Do you mind if I stay?" He addressed the last question to Analee and they both turned to Nora.

"You're right; Analee does need bolstering up this evening. Please, stay and enjoy. I must find Martin." Nora hurried off on her mission.

Analee stood beside Gus, suddenly mute. Nora's chatter had covered several awkward moments, but now she was alone. Her old fears returned. Gus sensed her withdrawal. "Shall we get some champagne?" he asked carefully. "I think they are serving in the next room."

Taking Analee's arm, they wound their way through the crowded room to the doorway. A bar and buffet had been set up in the dining room. The food was barely touched. The guests were not yet interested in eating.

Gus asked the bartender for champagne. Turning to Analee, he handed her a glass. "Cheers. Here's to our friend, Nora."

Analee sipped the wine. Gus was being so kind and thoughtful. Maybe it would be OK to go with him on a tour. And, there would be other people around.

Gus watched Analee's face. Her eyes were easy to read, and he was encouraged by what he saw in them. "Have you made a decision about touring with me? I overheard someone here talking about a castle tour. Would that interest you?"

Analee smiled bravely. "Nora had arranged for me to join someone named Margaret who is conducting a castle tour. I suppose that's who you heard."

"Let's go find her and see if there's room for one more." Gus took Analee's hand and started toward a small group surrounding a tall woman who was wearing a well-tailored, navy blue suit. Her blond hair was pulled back in a top knot. Her dark eyes snapped as she finished a story she was relating to the group.

Analee thought the woman was attractive but rather overbearing. If this was Margaret, she was probably a successful tour leader.

Gus parted the crowd with a quiet, "Excuse us, please," and drew Analee beside him. "Are you Margaret?" he smiled warmly at the women.

"I am. And you are --- ?"

"Gus Herman, and this is Analee Webster, Nora's friend from America. I gather you are taking a tour of English Castles."

Margaret held out her hand to Analee, and they shook hands.

"Nora has already booked you, Analee. I'm so pleased to meet you at last." She turned to Gus. "You are American as well? Also, a friend of Nora?"

"No, I've only just met her. I'm in London on business. My colleague, Elspeth Sheffield, invited me to this party. It seems she was unable to come after all."

"Oh Elspeth," Margaret laughed. "She's notorious for disappearing at the last minute. Don't be angry with her."

Gus smiled and drew Analee a little closer. "I'm anything but angry. I have found a friend and touring companion. That is, if you have room for one more on your tour?"

Margaret nodded eagerly. "Of course we do. I'll add your name to the roster. We can finalize the arrangements tomorrow. The tour departs from the Park Lane Hotel at 10 a.m. Sunday." She turned toward the door. "I have a few details to take care of. See you two on Sunday."

Analee and Gus watched her disappear through the door and turned to look at each other. Analee was thinking she should go back to Nora's and pack. She must move to the hotel tonight.

Gus was thinking he wanted to help Analee develop more confidence in herself. She was a lovely woman with much to offer. She just needed a boost, and he was just the man to give it to her.

Gus spoke first. "Let's find Nora, then go get your things. We'll get a taxi to take us to the Park Lane."

Analee found herself held closely by Gus and swept through the crowd. Nora gave them her key. They hurried down the steps of Martin's house into the square. Gus hailed a passing taxi and helped Analee into the spacious back seat.

Gus loved the London taxis, thinking they were very sensible vehicles.

He gave the driver Nora's address, and they drove away. Analee sat quietly with Gus; her mind swirling with everything happening. Nora's recital was tomorrow evening; then she and Gus would be leaving on Sunday for the Castle Tour. What followed that, she wasn't sure. The only sure thing was her growing dependence on Gus. He was so self-assured and strong- minded. She felt she could just put her life in his hands, and he would take care of her.

CHAPTER 6

The taxi drew up in front of Nora's house and Gus instructed the driver to wait. Analee hurried inside and quickly packed her things. She was back in the taxi with Gus in less than twenty minutes. The taxi sped off toward the Park Lane Hotel.

Gus sat close to Analee and watched her surreptitiously out of the corner of his eye. He wanted to know her better, what her inner thoughts were, what made her "tick." She was unlike any woman he had ever met. Maybe there was a possibility of a much closer relationship happening soon.

Analee was aware of Gus's scrutiny and tried not to let it bother her. In truth, he made her very nervous. What was he looking for? She knew very little about him, after all. Was she making another mistake in trusting him?

The smiling, uniformed Park Lane doorman opened the taxi door, beaming as they emerged. "Welcome to the Park Lane. I will see to your bags while you go to Reception, inside to your left."

Gus guided Analee through the door and down the steps to Reception. "Miss Webster's room, please." The clerk handed over a key card. "Room 402. Please let us know if you require anything. The porter will deliver your bags in a few minutes."

Analee turned to Gus as they walked to the lift. "I don't know how to thank you for taking care of me. I would have been on a plane home by now."

Gus took both her hands in his as he looked into her eyes. "You won't regret staying on, I promise. We'll have a wonderful tour with

Margaret. We'll know each other better in a few days." His thoughts were on just *how much better* they would know each other.

Analee couldn't speak. She could only nod. Gus's gaze was warm and knowing.

They reached Analee's room, and Gus opened the door for her. He turned on the lamps, checked the window locks and drew the drapes. "I'll wait until the porter brings your bags; in case you feel uncomfortable alone."

Analee was grateful for his concern and thoughtfulness. She would have been uneasy even though the hotel porters were undoubtedly trustworthy. Just then, a soft knock announced the arrival of the porter. Analee opened the door, and the young man entered. He set her bags down on the luggage rack, smiling as she thanked him with a proper tip.

She turned to Gus. "Thank you again. Will I see you tomorrow?"

"Oh yes. Breakfast at 8 – OK? I'll meet you downstairs. By the way, I am in 516 if you need to call me." Gus leaned over and kissed her cheek. "Goodnight, Lee" he said as he closed the door quietly.

* * * * *

Analee took a deep breath and slumped on the side of the bed. She was exhausted after the events of the day. She inspected the room and found it to her liking. It was impersonal, yet warm and inviting. The furniture was white, and the carpet dark blue. The bedspread and drapes were matching blue with white flowers. Rousing herself enough to take out her night clothes and toiletries, she prepared for bed. Just as she was turning down the bed, the telephone rang startling her.

"Hel-hello," Analee spoke uncertainly. Gus's deep voice was warm. "Just wanted to see if you're doing OK."

"Yes, I'm ready for sleep. How about you?"

"I'll probably read for a while. I usually do. Do you want me to call you in the morning, or leave a wake up call at the desk?"

"You can call me if you're up early enough."

"OK, I will. Goodnight then." Analee heard the click as Gus hung up.

True to his word, Gus rang the phone at 7 A.M. Analee was awake and answered cheerfully. "Good morning, Gus. Did you sleep well?"

Gus was encouraged by her bright tone of voice. "Yes I did. Are you ready for breakfast? They have good food here."

"Give me some time to put myself together," Analee giggled. "Aren't we meeting at 8?"

"Yes, I'll stop bothering you. See you at 8."

Analee was prompt, but Gus was already in the Garden Room when she arrived. The waiter hurried over with coffee as she took her seat.

"You look brand new," Gus said admiringly. "A good night's sleep does wonders for you."

Analee blushed and opened the menu. "I'll have the Continental Breakfast," she told the waiter softly.

Gus ordered porridge, and Analee looked questioningly at him. "It's oatmeal," Gus grinned. "When I'm in London, I like to call it porridge as they do. Makes me feel more British."

"Are you part British?"

"Yes, my ancestors were from England and Scotland. I have researched some of my heritage and find it fascinating. It's one reason why I want to take the Castle Tour with you. There may be more ancestry I can discover."

"That's very interesting" Analee looked thoughtful. "I don't think my family has ever been traced. We're just plain Americans."

"Most people can find ancestors from Europe if they go back far enough."

Before Analee could comment further, the waiter carefully placed her breakfast in front of her. Gus's oatmeal arrived, and they began eating.

Just then, a strident female voice was heard at the entrance to the dining room. "Gus, my dear, there you are!" Elspeth Sheffield fairly blazed a path through the room.

Her outfit today was a black wool suit, worn with chunky gold jewelry. Her ubiquitous mink coat trailed behind her. The maitre d' rushed to catch it. Elspeth reached the table and signaled the waiter for coffee.

"Good morning, Analee," she said coolly as she sat down.

Analee could barely whisper a reply. Why was this woman here?

Gus was as puzzled as Analee was. He half rose from his chair as Elspeth joined them. "I thought you were in Spain."

"That was yesterday," Elspeth said quickly. "I returned early this morning. Are you free today? There are some details we should complete as soon as possible."

Gus glanced quickly at Analee. "We were about to discuss our plans. Nora's recital is tonight, and I planned to show Analee a little of London today."

Elspeth's eyes narrowed and focused on Analee. "She's an adult. There are sightseeing tours available. I need you *today,* Gus!"

Analee was completely at a loss to understand the change in Elspeth. Her manner was entirely different from before. Was she jealous? Did Gus belong to her?

Gus turned to Analee. "Would you mind terribly if we didn't sightsee today? I really should conclude my business with Elspeth."

"No, of course not." Analee spoke clearly. "I can amuse myself for a few hours." She certainly didn't want Elspeth to think she was holding on to Gus.

"I'll be back in time to escort you to Nora's recital," Gus promised as he stood up.

Elspeth's triumphant smile did not reach her eyes. She took Gus's arm. They strode to the door; Analee's eyes following them.

Analee finished her coffee, signed the bill, and left the dining room. The maitre d' smiled sympathetically as she passed. Her face felt hot. She imagined everyone was staring at her. She hurried to the elevator and punched #4, but before the door closed, a hand reached out to hold the door. Analee jumped back into the corner and held her breath. Two large men, speaking rapidly to each other, entered the lift. One of them punched #3. Analee let out her breath. At least, they were getting off before her floor. Her bravado with Gus and Elspeth was rapidly disappearing. She would probably spend the day in her room, reading a book.

When she was safely in her room, she sat down to think. This trip was turning more corners than a maze. Was Gus really interested in her? What did Elspeth's attitude mean? Where was Nora, now that she needed her?

As if on cue, the telephone rang. Analee sprang up to answer it.

"Hello, love!" Nora's voice came over the line. "We're just checking the arrangements for tonight. I wanted to see how you are doing today. Did you get settled in? Is Gus with you?" Her questions came rapidly.

Analee gripped the phone. "Yes, I'm settled in. Gus and I had breakfast; then Elspeth claimed him for some business. I'm on my own until tonight."

"Oh, you poor thing!" Nora exclaimed. "What are your plans?"

"I really don't know yet. I'm just trying to sort things out."

"Well, I'm sure you'll be fine. Shopping is good near the hotel, if you feel like walking around. Just go straight down Piccadilly, and you will find interesting shops." Nora breezily instructed. "Oh, by the way, I have left two tickets at the box office for you and Gus for the recital. I'll see you afterwards."

"OK Nora, and thanks."

"Bye now." Nora clicked off.

CHAPTER 7

Analee felt better and decided to go out for a while. Nora always had that effect on her. She was cheerful and positive, something Analee lacked most of the time. Gathering her jacket and purse, Analee left the room and made her way to the lobby. The lobby was empty, and she pushed through the revolving door to the street. A brisk walk would do her good, she thought, and gazed around at all the sights as she set out.

Green Park was across the street and another small hotel sat next door to the Park Lane. She walked on down the street, enjoying the sights. When she came to an arcade, she slowed, visually devouring all the displays in the shop windows. Continuing to browse, she arrived at *Fortnum and Mason* and went in. This store was famous for fancy and specialty foods. She wanted to see inside. In the rear of the store, there was a small tea room. By this time, she was ready for some lunch. Analee timidly approached the line for seating. Hoping there was a table in the corner, she waited her turn.

The two women just behind Analee were discussing someone's love life. Analee did not want to eavesdrop, but the women were speaking loudly. The subject seemed to be the latest conquest of their boss. Analee heard "Corporate Suites" and "Sheffield," then "Gus Herman." She realized they were discussing Elspeth and Gus as a romantic connection. The next words she heard came crashing down on her ears with such force that she almost staggered:

"Elspeth told me she was going to have him, and that Nora's friend was leaving for America. Elspeth is ruthless if she wants something or someone."

The other girl nodded. "I know she is. I pity the American girl."

Analee could not take any more and pushed past the waiting line, fleeing the store. She ran, sobbing, back to the hotel and her room. What kind of game was Gus playing? She had begun to trust him and now this.

Analee huddled in a chair; her mind whirling. She could never trust Gus again. How could she spend five days touring with him? As her eyes darted around the room, she finally focused on a red light on the telephone. A message! She picked up the receiver and dialed the operator. The message was from Gus, saying his business was taking more time than he originally planned, and she should go on to the recital. He would join her later. Elspeth seemed to be carrying out the words Analee heard earlier. Would Gus show up at all?

After awhile, Analee pulled herself together and dressed for the recital. Her simple black dress was beautifully cut, needing no more than a strand of pearls for adornment. She slipped into black, strappy high-heeled sandals, picked up her evening bag, and descended to the lobby. She was determined to get through the evening somehow and show Gus he could choose Elspeth if he wanted to.

The doorman signaled a taxi and helped Analee enter. "Queen Elizabeth Hall" she told the driver, and the cab sped off.

* * * * *

Queen Elizabeth Hall was in the Covent Garden area of London, an area Analee wanted to explore someday. "If only Nora had kept her promise," Analee thought, "we would be planning our itinerary instead of going our separate ways."

Analee stepped out of the taxi in front of the Hall and hesitated, her eyes searching the building for the ticket window. There were few people around since it was early yet for the crowd to arrive. A kindly looking security guard stood near a door. Analee started toward him to ask directions. The guard indicated a glassed-in window along the inside wall where Analee could pick up her ticket. She told the clerk to hold the other one in case Mr. Herman arrived later.

Since it was early, Analee wondered if she should try to find

Nora. She wandered through the lobby looking for the stage door.

At the far end of the lobby, a door opened and a blond head poked cautiously out. Nora hissed, "Analee – over here."

Analee turned at the sound and smiled with relief. "Nora! How are you feeling? Are you nervous?"

"Oh yes, of course I'm nervous." Nora chuckled, "but I'll be fine. Where's Gus?"

Analee ducked her head. "I don't know if he's coming."

Nora looked puzzled. "What happened? Did you quarrel?"

"It's a long story," Analee mumbled. "I'll tell you later."

"Well, I've got to go warm up and change." Nora turned quickly, and as the door closed, Analee heard, "See you after the recital." She was alone again, but the lobby was beginning to fill with music lovers.

Analee took out her ticket and headed for the ushers at the door to the Hall. She might as well sit down.

* * * * *

Nora's recital was brilliant, and she received a standing ovation. Analee was so proud of her friend, though not surprised. She always knew Nora's talent was a true gift.

A reception was being held in one of the public rooms. By the time Analee reached it, Nora was surrounded by well-wishers and admirers. Analee stood on the fringe, waiting until the crowd thinned before approaching Nora. At last, the admirers drifted away, still chatting among themselves about the remarkable talent they had heard tonight.

Analee reached Nora and hugged her warmly. "You were wonderful," she breathed. "I knew you would be."

"Thanks love, but I'm glad it's over. Where's Martin?"

"I saw him when I came in." Analee glanced around the room. "Over there by the champagne."

"Of course, he would be." Nora laughed as she started toward Martin. "Come on, let's have a glass ourselves."

Analee followed Nora across the room and accepted a glass of champagne from a waiter.

"A toast to Nora!" someone in the crowd called out. "Cheers!"

sounded the gathered throng. Nora lifted her glass in delighted acceptance, and everyone sipped his drink.

Analee watched as Nora and Martin gazed adoringly at each other. She felt rather lonely at that moment, when she had hoped to be here with Gus. She was still lost in thought when a voice behind her whispered, "Analee?"

She turned so quickly that her face almost collided with Gus's chin. She blushed in embarrassment. Before she could speak, Gus said, "I'm sorry I missed Nora's performance. It must have been wonderful from what I'm hearing."

Analee nodded, unable to speak. Her eyes filled with tears as she struggled to regain control. Gus wanted to spare her further embarrassment, so he took her arm and led her to the side of the room. Analee found her voice.

"Where are you taking me? Is Elspeth waiting for you? I don't want to detain you." She lifted her chin and looked up at Gus. "You certainly needn't feel obligated to me or Nora. I can take care of myself now."

Gus frowned. Why was Analee turning away? She had been so dependent on him.

Nora and Martin strolled over and greeted Gus. "There you are. We were afraid you had missed the performance." Martin beamed and held up Nora's hand. "She's wonderful, isn't she?"

Gus smiled at them. "I'm afraid I did miss it, and I apologize. I've heard you dazzled everyone, Nora."

"Thank you, you're very kind. But what detained you?"

"Business, I'm afraid, and Elspeth's timing." Gus hoped Analee accepted his answer. There was more he needed to discuss with her.

Martin glanced at his watch. "Nora, my dear, we must go change and pack. Our flight to Paris leaves at midnight." They blew kisses at everyone as they hurried away.

Nora called out to Analee, "I'll ring you when we get settled in Paris."

Analee and Gus were left standing alone. Analee was uneasy, unsure of herself and the situation. Gus took charge. "I'll see you back to the hotel. We can get a cab out front." He took Analee's arm, and they walked out together.

In the cab, Gus turned to Analee. "My business here has taken an unexpected turn. I won't be able to take the Castle Tour with you. I do hope you understand."

"Of course," Analee said stiffly. "You must take care of business first."

"When will you return to the States?"

"As soon as the tour ends, I'll be flying home. There is no need to stay longer."

"Maybe I'll see you in Bloomington some day," Gus ventured, not sure of his welcome, but Analee smiled faintly.

"Perhaps" was her soft reply.

At the Park Lane Gus helped Analee alight from the taxi and walked her to the lift. "Will you be all right from here? Someone is waiting for me in the bar."

Analee was trying hard to control her voice, but it quavered as she said, "Yes, I'm fine. Goodbye, Gus."

The elevator door slid shut. Analee slumped against the wall. She felt deserted and afraid. Could she get through the next few days?

* * * * *

Gus stood for a moment after the lift doors were closed, musing about the frightened girl he had just seen and her words to him. "Goodbye Gus," she had said, not "Goodnight." It was so final, he thought. He was attracted to her and had hoped their time together on the tour would help Analee open herself to him. He wanted to learn more about her, and possibly arrange a sexual liaison, too!

"Damn Elspeth" he thought to himself. "She has other plans for my time in the guise of business."

Elspeth waited for Gus in the Lobby Bar. She had watched the farewell at the lift and knew Gus was struggling with himself. *Well, he could forget that little nobody Analee. She, Elspeth, was much better suited to him and was about to prove it.*

Gus came in and sat down heavily in the wingback chair across from Elspeth.

"Duty done?" Elspeth inquired sweetly. "She'll be fine, you know. Margaret will be a fine companion."

Gus nodded. "I know, but I still feel responsible. She's so

vulnerable and alone."

"Have a drink. We have many details to discuss." Elspeth sipped her wine and smiled across at Gus. She would keep him busy. He could forget little Analee.

CHAPTER 8

In her room, Analee tried to forget about Gus. "This trip has been nothing like I planned," she thought. "I'll try to enjoy the castle tour and fly home. Then my life will be back to normal." She packed everything except what she needed for the morning, and slid between the turned down sheets. The chocolate mint left on her pillow tasted good. She remembered that she hadn't eaten all day. No wonder the candy was so tasty. She must get up in time to have breakfast or she would probably faint.

Analee remembered fainting once when she was a little girl. Her parents had taken her to visit relatives who lived several hours away by car. She hadn't eaten breakfast, and before they could order lunch, Analee fainted in the restaurant. Her parents were frantic with worry about her. She remembered being revived with hot tea, and the day continued without further incident. She didn't want another episode like that to happen, calling attention to herself. She would rather blend in with the crowd.

Analee lay in bed, trying to go to sleep. Her mind was spinning with "Whys."

Why did Nora have to leave her?

Why did Gus take an interest?

Why did Elspeth want Gus?

Why was she missing Gus?

There it was! She missed Gus already. He had become important to her and she barely knew him. There was something so warm and trusting in his concern for her. She had never known a man like him.

But deep down inside she felt a little uneasy about his intentions,

Truth be known, she had never had a male friend before. All her college acquaintances were so juvenile. They were immature and focused on making conquests, not anything long term. She was determined to wait for a committed relationship.

Analee slept fitfully with her brain unwilling to let go of the troubling thoughts. When she awakened, she felt as if her body belonged to someone else, that someone being very old and tired. Her active brain, however, was commanding her body to perform its usual functions.

She showered and dressed quickly, packing the remainder of her things. She would have time for breakfast before meeting Margaret and the tour group.

The Garden Room was nearly empty. Analee was shown to a table along the wall. "On your own today, ma'am?" the host inquired politely. Analee nodded as she seated herself and glanced around the room. The other occupants were a young couple so engrossed in each other that they didn't notice anyone else.

Analee ordered coffee and a muffin, hoping her empty stomach would accept the food. Her emotions were upsetting everything today. As she was finishing her breakfast, she heard loud voices in the lobby just outside the dining room. Someone was very unhappy from the sound of it.

After signing the bill, Analee quickly left the room. More people were coming in and she felt conspicuous being alone. When she reached the lobby, Margaret was attempting to placate a very large woman who was screaming at her.

"I am very sorry, Mrs. Gray, but I cannot refund your money today. It will come from the main office in a few days."

The woman, red faced and sputtering, continued to screech that she needed the money now and was calling the authorities to help her.

Margaret spied Analee and winked at her. "Please do whatever you think best," she told the woman, "but you will find that I am advising you correctly."

Mrs. Gray turned and steamed out the door, leaving Margaret smirking and Analee staring. "You handled her very well, and I am impressed," Analee said.

Margaret raised her eyebrows at Analee. "When you have dealt with people as long as I have, you learn to defuse them if you can. She was all smoke and steam. Now, let's get our group sorted out. Are you all ready?"

Yes, as soon as I can get my bags from my room and check out," Analee said as she signaled the porter.

"Very well, then. The others are already on the bus. Come along when you finish."

The bus was idling at the curb on the Piccadilly side of the hotel. Analee stepped aboard and quickly evaluated the other passengers. To her dismay they were all in two's, chatting gaily together in eager anticipation of the tour.

Margaret had been conversing with the driver and boarded the bus just behind Analee. "Here, sit up front with me," she offered. "It's too bad your friend Gus had to cancel, leaving you alone."

Analee was surprised. "Y-You know?" she stammered.

"Yes, he rang me late yesterday. But don't worry, we'll have a bloody good time anyway."

As the coach rolled through London, Margaret began to outline the tour. She explained that technically, it was not all castles but included stately historic homes as well. The first stop was Windsor Castle, the official home of Her Majesty, the Queen. It is the largest inhabited castle in the world, begun over 900 years ago by William The Conqueror. When the Queen is in residence, the flag is flown from the tower and the castle is closed to visitors. Touring the grounds is allowed.

* * * * *

Waddesdon Manor, near Alyesbury in Buckinghamshire, was commissioned in the 18th century by Baron Ferdinand de Rothschild, a Frenchman who felt he needed a chateau within handy reach of his banking interests in London. Analee was beginning to like the tour and Margaret's ongoing explanations. The tour continued into Kent, to Knole, the largest private house in England. It is said to have a room for every day of the year.

The tour stopped for the night at a country inn called *The Royal, an 18th century 3-star hotel.* Dinner was in the Boathouse Bar. The tour group enjoyed a festive evening. Analee found she was very happy with her decision to take this tour.

The next day brought them to Leeds Castle. Analee was enchanted to see this fairy-tale castle. It is built on two islands in the middle of a lake. Many consider it the most beautiful castle in England. Analee certainly thought so. The tour of Leeds Castle extended almost to lunch time, and Margaret directed them to *The Black Horse Inn.* It was another charming place near the castle. This was a typical country pub with friendly service and unique charm. The menu was roast beef, Yorkshire pudding with apple crumble for dessert. Again, the tour group enjoyed the experience.

The tour continued on to Oxfordshire where they found Blenheim Palace. This was Winston Churchill's birthplace and contained a splendid Churchill exhibition. Blenheim is the only non-royal, non-Episcopal country house to hold the title of "Palace." It is also a World Heritage Site, and was home to the 12th Duke and Duchess of Marlborough. The group learned about Sir Winston Churchill's life and his connection to Blenheim Palace. They were treated to an exclusive look at the Duke's private apartments, and a State Room Tour included portraits, tapestries and furniture. A tour of the downstairs servants' quarters showed the group where there were 102 servants when the staff was largest. In World War II the staff was the smallest and the palace was temporarily a convalescent hospital.

Their next stop was Chatsworth House in Derbyshire. This historic, massive edifice has been home to the Duke of Devonshire since the 17th Century. It took nearly 200 years to complete.

The tour continued on past Sandringham House in Norfolk. This is the Queen's private estate with 20,000 acres of land. No tours are allowed here, and Margaret brought the tour group to The Dukes Head Hotel in Kings Lynn, not far from Sandringham. This inn was built in 1689, located in the market square. Princess Victoria stopped here in September 1835. After an excellent dinner in Turners Restaurant, they spent the night.

Near the end of the tour, Analee found herself exhausted from all the history and scenery she had seen. After a leisurely breakfast, the group boarded the bus for the return trip to London.

Margaret was true to her word. Analee *did* enjoy the tour. She even made friends with a man and woman who were from Cincinnati, almost neighbors from the Midwest. Analee felt reluctant to leave Margaret and her new friends. Now, she was on her own again for the flight home.

* * * * *

The 747 was crowded, but Analee's seat in first class was comfortable and spacious. If she could always fly first class, she wouldn't mind traveling alone. But that was a dream not likely to come true.

The flight was smooth and uneventful, no Gus to make it exciting or even interesting. The flight attendant served a delicious four-course meal; then the passengers lowered their window shades for the movie. Analee felt removed from it all. Her anticipation for the trip had waned, all the broken promises littering her memory.

CHAPTER 9

B ack in Bloomington, Analee threw herself into her work at the restaurant. She needed to forget whatever her feelings were for Gus. She was very confused about the matter. There was much to learn, and her father was a patient teacher. He gave her increasing responsibility, advising and counseling through it all. Analee had many ideas to try out on him.

Isaac Webster was proud of his daughter and her creative mind. He did worry about her social life or lack thereof. It seemed to him that Analee was unhappy somehow; although when he confronted her, she denied it. Putting on a bright face, she would pat his cheek and chirp, "Daddy, you're seeing things that aren't there. I am fine, happy, and enjoy being with you."

Isaac and Analee's mother Mabel, discussed Analee one evening in the kitchen as they finished dinner. "Has Analee said any more about Nora?" Isaac questioned. "Has she heard from her since returning from London?"

Mabel shook her head. "No, there have been no letters or calls that I know of. Do you think Analee is worried about Nora?"

"I just don't know, but something is bothering our girl. She's just not happy."

They sat over coffee; each lost in thought and concern about Analee.

The family home was a large, two-story house on a quiet, tree-lined street. Analee loved every inch of her home from the farthest corner of the attic to the large finished basement. Her childhood had been spent roaming the many rooms, imagining herself a princess in a castle or a wealthy businesswoman in high society.

Peter, her older brother, had moved out while Analee was in high school and now lived and worked in California. Peter never seemed a part of the family somehow. He was brash, breezy and fun loving. He stopped at home barely long enough to say "hello." Isaac and Mabel just shook their heads when Peter was mentioned. They could only hope he would remember his roots someday.

Now, Analee found her refuge in the comfortable, old house. It felt warm and welcoming each time she returned. If she stopped to think about Gus or Nora, she became morose and unhappy, so she filled the hours and days with work and tried not to remember.

Several of her girl friends in town had invited her to lunch, dinner, or a drink after work, wanting to hear all about Analee's trip. But, Analee had politely put them off, using the excuse that the restaurant was keeping her too busy. Brenda, her best friend, would not be put off. Analee finally confided in her, pouring out the whole story including her confusion over Gus.

Brenda was sympathetic. "You'll hear from Gus again. He sounds like an honorable man to me."

"I wish I could be sure," Analee sighed. "After Nora's surprise marriage, I felt deserted and betrayed. If Gus breaks his promise, I'll never trust a man again."

Brenda glared at her friend. "You just haven't met the right man yet. Don't lump all males into one category. There are good ones, you know."

"I suppose so. Thanks for listening to my tale of woe."

"It's what I do best." Brenda smiled.

* * * * *

A few weeks later Analee was busy in the office at *Henry's*, making up a new menu. A light tap on the doorframe drew her attention to a man standing in the doorway. The man was short, stocky, with black hair combed straight back. His dark, snapping eyes crinkled at the corners. He was smiling at Analee as she said, "Hello, may I help you with something?"

"My name is Dak Brown with Restaurant Supply." He held out

a business card. "We have a new line of products I'd like to show you."

"Please sit down." Analee invited. "I'm not sure we need anything, but I'll be glad to look over your catalog." She glanced at his card. "Your name is unusual. Is Dak a nickname?"

"It's short for Dakota," he chuckled. "My mom thought North Dakota was a place to remember since I was born there." Dak spread out his catalogs and brochures, and they began to discuss the products.

Two hours later, Isaac entered the restaurant to the sound of laughter coming from Analee's office. He paused, listened, and thought it had been ages since he had heard his daughter laugh. As he drew closer, he realized the cause of the hilarity came from a deep, rumbling male voice telling jokes. And Analee was convulsed with giggles. Seeking to learn the identity of this man, Isaac stepped into Analee's office. "Hi, how's it going?"

"Oh, hello Dad" Analee gasped, wiping her eyes. "Dak knows some really funny stories."

Isaac stretched out his hand as the younger man rose. "Dak, is it?" he asked.

"Yes, Dak Brown with Restaurant Supply." The men shook hands, and Isaac glanced at the material spread out on Analee's desk.

"Have you made any decisions, Lee?"

"No, Dad, I was sidetracked by the stories Dak was telling. Do you want to look over the catalogs?"

"Not now. If you see something we should consider, let me know. I'll be in the kitchen."

Isaac left them alone, and Analee felt the atmosphere change. She had never been so at ease with a man before. Dak was so easy to talk with. He made her feel witty and feminine all at once. His humor, mostly directed at himself, was refreshing.

Dak himself was smitten. One look at Analee and he was in love. She was the intelligent, sweet, shy female of his dreams. And, she laughed at his jokes!

"Do you ever leave this place?" Dak inquired.

Analee raised her eyebrows. "Leave? What do you mean?"

"For lunch, or dinner, or anything." Dak leaned over the desk. "Will you have dinner with me – somewhere else?"

Analee considered this man looking at her so intensely. Her eyes locked on his, and she felt breathless as if she had been running a long time. Neither one could look away for several seconds. "Will you please?" Dak whispered at last.

"Yes," Analee whispered back. "When and where?"

"Tonight, seven o'clock. I'll call for you. Tell me where you live."

"296 Oakmont, my home. I want you to meet my mother, too." Analee felt hypnotized. These things didn't happen to her.

* * * * *

Precisely at 7:00 p.m., the doorbell rang at 296 Oakmont. Isaac and Mabel were sitting in the living room, having been informed by a glowing Analee that she had a date.

Isaac ambled to the door. "Come in, Dak. Analee will be down soon."

Dak stepped into the wide entry hall, noting the curving staircase rising to the second floor, the oak paneling and polished banister. "My dream home," he thought, as Isaac guided him through the archway on the left. Mabel stood in front of her wingback chair, curious about this male person who put stars in her daughter's eyes.

"Mabel, this is Dak Brown." Isaac's voice boomed across the room. "He was in the restaurant today representing Restaurant Supply."

"I'm pleased to meet you." Mabel felt her fingers clasped in Dak's large, warm hand and experienced the same surge of hypnotism as had Analee.

Dak's eyes swept over Mabel and took in the entire room, while fixing her with his intense gaze. Mabel immediately knew what had attracted her daughter to this man. He exuded sexuality!

"Please, sit down. Analee will be along soon. May I get you a drink?" Mabel babbled the words as Isaac sent her a questioning look. What was going on with his women?

Dak lowered himself into the other wingback chair, thinking Analee's mother a charming woman. Analee promised to be just like her when she "grew up."

"Nothing for me, thanks," Dak answered Mabel.

"Where do you live, Dak?" Isaac began, intending to learn more about this hypnotic man.

"In Chicago, for the time being," Dak answered "but I'm to be transferred soon, and it may be to Cincinnati. My territory includes the southern part of the state, so Cincinnati will be a better location.

"Will your territory expand as well?" Mabel interjected.

"Yes, I will be covering three states."

The three of them heard Analee's step on the stairs and turned to watch her enter the room. She blushed as she saw them.

"Hello Dak," she said softly. "You found our house OK?"

Analee picked up her jacket, and Dak rushed to help her put it on. "You look gorgeous," he whispered close to her ear. Analee blushed again and turned to her parents. "We won't be late. Don't wait up."

Dak shook hands again with both Isaac and Mabel. "I'll take good care of her and bring her back safely," he promised.

CHAPTER 10

D ak's car was a small station wagon loaded with sample books and catalogs. He had cleared the front seat and now helped Analee into it. He climbed into the driver's seat and they sped off.

"I noticed a little inn on the edge of town and checked to see if they serve dinner. How does that sound?" Dak inquired.

"*The Talbot House?*"

"Yes, that's the one. OK?"

At Analee's nod, Dak drove swiftly through town, arriving at the *Talbot House* in a few minutes. They had both been silent during the drive, each wondering how the evening would turn out. A parking attendant took the car at the entrance. Dak escorted Analee up the steps to the carved, heavy door.

"Have you been here before?" Dak inquired.

"Only once, when I was a senior in high school. My best friend's parents brought us here to celebrate our being named to the National Honor Society. We had a very nice dinner."

Dak held the door open for Analee to enter the dark interior. A small woman stood behind the podium.

"Good evening. Do you have a reservation?"

"The name is Brown, for two."

The woman looked down at the list on the podium and marked off the name. Smiling, she picked up two menus and motioned for them to follow her. Their table was in a cozy corner, lit by a candle on the table, and a small, dim lamp on a stand nearby. "Just right," thought Dak, as he held Analee's chair, then seated himself.

Two hours later, Analee looked at her watch and gasped. "Why, it's ten o'clock. No wonder the place is almost empty. They want to close!"

Dak leaned his chin on his hand and gazed across the table. "We just got here, didn't we? The evening has flown by."

"I know," said Analee picking up her purse. "It has gone fast, but I think we should go. The staff needs to finish up. Believe me, they don't appreciate lingerers."

"OK then." Dak stood up and took Analee's elbow to guide her through the maze of tables. She felt his hand on her arm, warm and steady.

Back on Oakmont, Dak stopped in front of the Webster house and turned off the motor. They sat for a moment before Dak turned to Analee.

"I'll be back in this area in two weeks. May I see you again?"

Analee smiled at him. "Yes, I think that would be wonderful. I had a good time tonight. You are very entertaining."

Dak took her hand and leaned toward her, whispering, "Since the porch light is on, may I kiss you goodnight out here?"

Analee's eyes widened, and her face felt hot, but she nodded. Dak's lips were soft and moist as they touched her warm mouth. The kiss lasted only seconds, but to Analee the world stopped in those seconds.

Dak's eyes opened, and he looked deeply into Analee's eyes. "Goodnight Princess," he murmured. "I'll see you in two weeks."

He came around the car and opened Analee's door. She stepped out of the car into Dak's arms. They stood wrapped in an embrace for a long moment; then, Dak drew back, took Analee's hand and slowly walked her to the door.

"It has been a memorable evening." Dak began. "I don't want it to end."

"I know, me too." Analee could hardly speak. They stood holding hands in front of the door.

They might have stood there for hours had not the door been opened by Isaac whose voice broke the spell. "I hate to break this up, but Analee has a phone call. It's Nora, calling from Paris."

Analee jumped and ran inside to the telephone. Isaac and Dak were left standing in the doorway. "Do you want to come in for a minute, Dak?" Isaac held the door open.

"No, I need to be going. Tell Analee I'll call her tomorrow."
"I'll do that. Goodnight, Dak." Isaac closed the door as Dak went down the steps to his car.

* * * * *

Analee sat by the telephone for a few minutes after her conversation with Nora. Her friend had called with disturbing news. Martin was very ill and in a Paris hospital. Nora was alone and frightened. The prognosis for his recovery was guarded. If and when he could be released from the hospital, his recovery would be very slow with skilled care necessary. Analee wondered how she could help Nora and Martin.

Isaac found his daughter slumped by the telephone, head in hands. "What's wrong, honey? Is Nora OK?"

"Oh Dad, it's Martin, Nora's new husband. He's very ill, and I don't know what to do."

Isaac pulled her to her feet and put his arm around her shoulders. "Go to bed now. You'll be able to think more clearly tomorrow. Things always look brighter in daylight."

Analee started up the stairs and turned to her father. "Did Dak leave?"

"Yes, he said he would call tomorrow."

Analee smiled and continued up the stairs to her room. Later, when she was in bed, she remembered every detail of the evening with Dak. He was a sweet, charming man and had captivated her with his spell. Her feelings for him were hopeful. Never before had a relationship come this far. She didn't want to do anything to scare him away, at least not until they both had a chance to explore this new friendship.

* * * * *

The next morning was a busy one for Analee and Isaac. They interviewed several applicants for wait staff jobs, mostly college students seeking to augment their spending money. They were finishing with the last applicant when the phone rang.

"*Henry's,*" Analee spoke quickly into the phone.

"You sound very businesslike," came Dak's voice. "Are you tied up at the moment?"

"N-no, I can talk. How are you?"

Isaac motioned that he was leaving with the girl they had just interviewed, and closed the door.

"The question is, how are you? When I left last night, you seemed upset. Is everything all right?" Dak sounded anxious and concerned.

Analee sighed and explained about Nora and Martin. "I don't know how I can help Nora, but I wish I could do something."

"Tough situation," Dak agreed. "I thought about you all night." Dak's voice became soft and sweet. "Are you free today at all? Can we spend a few minutes together before I leave?"

Analee took a deep breath. "I'll have to see what Dad's doing. If he can cover for me, I can get away for an hour."

"Great! I'll come right over and hope for the best," and he hung up.

Analee went in search of her father, smiling to herself. Isaac noting the happy face quickly agreed to mind the store. Analee raced to the ladies' room to freshen up.

Dak arrived in record time. He stood in the door to Analee's office as she came out of the ladies' room. "Hi, Princess," he said and took her hands in his. Smiling, they stood as if mesmerized, eyes locked together.

"Let's get out of here." Dak broke the spell, pulling her out the door to his car. "Where can we go and talk?"

Dak started the car and drove slowly out of the parking lot. He was still holding her hand.

"Maybe the park would be a good place." Analee pointed the way and the station wagon was soon in the city park. "There's a small lake over there. We can find a bench." Analee got out of the car as Dak came around. He grabbed her hand, and they ran like children laughing as they went.

The bench they found was in a little arbor, making it private and secluded. Dak pulled Analee down beside him and put his arm around her. "You have cast a spell over me," he murmured. "Women don't usually get to me very much."

Analee was captivated even more. "I feel the same about you," she whispered. "It's you who has cast the spell."

Dak's smile was warm. "I was hoping to hear you say that. I think there is hope for our future."

"Yes, I think we need to see what happens. But let's go slowly. This is all new to me."

"OK, Princess," Dak said jauntily. "It will be slow because I can't be here with you all the time. My business will keep me away from you. But, I'll call so you won't forget me."

They sat watching the wind blow ruffles on the lake's surface. The sun was warm on their faces. Analee could see deep into Dak's eyes. She saw no shadows or grief, only happiness and joy. This man was special. Maybe she could finally develop a relationship with a man. Maybe her luck was about to change.

CHAPTER II

When she came back to *Henry's,* her father was waiting, face set in a worried frown. "Nora phoned again. Martin is being moved to a private hospital in London. She's having to give up her music studies. I think you should call her. She needs a friendly voice right now."

Analee hurried to her desk and quickly punched the number Isaac handed her. Nora's voice was soft and quivery when she answered.

"Nora, it's Lee. I'm so sorry. What a rotten deal."

"Oh, Lee, I'm so glad you rang. It's very selfish, but I need you. Could you possibly pop over to London and help me? You understand me better than anyone. It is very difficult for my associates to comprehend the situation with Martin. They have never been faced with an invalid spouse."

Analee drew a deep breath. "You're asking a lot, Nora."

"I know, love, but will you think about it, please? Your presence would mean so much to me."

Analee promised to let her know in a couple of days and hung up the phone. She covered her face with her hands and thought, "Why now? Just as my life is coming together with the promise of a relationship with Dak. It's not fair!"

Isaac strode into the office, noting Analee's slumping posture. "What's wrong? Is Martin worse?"

Analee uncovered her face and sighed. "Nora wants me to come and help her in London. Martin will be a patient in a private hospital, and she has no other help. I don't know what to do."

Isaac sat down across from his daughter. "If you feel you can make Nora's life easier and help her adjust, go ahead. I can manage here for a few weeks. After all, I've been at it for quite a while," he smiled.

"Oh, Dad, you are the best! I need to mull it over a little while before I make a decision. But, Nora pleads a powerful case."

That night in bed, Analee lay thinking. She liked the feeling of being needed by Nora and by Isaac. Then, there was Dak. He would be calling, and she might be gone. Would he lose interest? Their relationship was so new and fragile. So many decisions – she was getting a headache.

The next day was Saturday and *Henry's* was busy all day. The lunch crowd came early and stayed late, leaving no gap before the normal Saturday evening rush. Isaac and Analee hardly spoke except in passing, each busy with their respective duties.

As the last diner paid his bill and left, Isaac locked the door and leaned against it for a minute. "Wow! What a night!" he exclaimed. "I'm glad you were here, Lee. It made a huge difference."

Analee smiled ruefully. "And, you say you can get along without me. Are you sure?"

"Yes, ma'am," he said emphatically. It's great to have you here, but if you can help Nora, don't worry about me."

They linked arms and went in search of a cup of coffee before closing up. The wait staff was almost finished.

"Dad, what should I do?" Analee stirred her coffee slowly and watched it swirl gently in the cup.

"I can't tell you what to do, honey. But, what about Dak? What happens if you go away? Will he understand?"

Analee shook her head. "I don't know. This is all new to me. Dak's reaction is a mystery."

"Obviously, Nora believes you can drop everything and fly to her side with no consequences," Isaac said thoughtfully. "Your situation is somewhat unique; it's true."

Analee sipped her coffee slowly. "I think I have to go help Nora," she sighed. "What kind of friend would I be if I didn't go?"

Isaac leaned over and kissed his daughter's cheek. "I'm proud of you; whatever you decide. Now, let's go home. It's late."

On Sunday, *Henry's* opened at 5:00 p.m. for the dinner hour, so Analee and Isaac had a few hours to relax. Mabel and Isaac usually attended church, and Sunday lunch was a roast left cooking while they were gone.

Analee awakened late after her parents had gone. She stretched lazily, sniffing the aroma of roasting meat, and felt peaceful. Her world was upright and orderly, the way she liked it. Her decision to go to England meant an upset to the order, but she knew Nora needed her. Later, she would call Dak and explain.

She threw back the covers and slid out of bed. The sunshine drew her to the window, and she stood observing the trees and flowers in the back yard. Her favorite tree was a tall, sturdy maple with thick limbs that still held her rope swing. Isaac made sure it was safe each spring, and Analee still loved to sit and swing.

Turning slowly from the window, Analee began to plan for the trip she must take. First, she would call TWA and book a flight. Then, she would call Nora to advise her arrival. Her clothes would not be a problem since she had barely worn the new things she had for the first trip.

Analee showered and dressed and was downstairs reading the paper when Mabel and Isaac came in. Mabel hugged her daughter.

"Dad told me your decision is to go to see Nora again" she exclaimed. "I'm so proud that you're willing to help your friend. Just don't stay away too long, or your young man may get restless!"

Analee smiled at her mother. "I know, Mom, and I'm hoping Dak will understand. If I can reach him today, I'll try to explain."

Mabel bustled out of the room to change and finish lunch. She called over her shoulder, "Brenda was at church, and I invited her for lunch."

Mabel was always picking up strays and inviting them home. Brenda was a frequent visitor, almost family to Isaac and Mabel. Isaac sat in his recliner with the sports section of the newspaper, listening indulgently to Mabel's comments.

At the sound of the doorbell, Analee rose quickly to admit Brenda. The two girls hugged, and Brenda spoke. "You look happy today. Have you had good news or something?"

Analee linked arms with Brenda and walked her into the living room. "Dad, here's Brenda."

Isaac peered over the paper and smiled. "So she is. Hello again."

The two girls sat on the sofa as Analee began to tell her friend the latest happenings. Brenda was surprised that Analee was going back to England so soon. "But what about Dak? Will he wait for you?" Brenda questioned.

"I don't know, but if he is the man I think he is, then yes, he'll understand. I plan to call him later today."

Mabel announced lunch, and they went into the dining room for the meal.

* * * * *

Isaac left for *Henry's* at 4:00 p.m., telling Analee to stay home if she wanted to. He felt he could manage the Sunday evening diners. Brenda left at the same time, saying she had laundry to do at home. Analee was grateful for her Dad's thoughtfulness since there was much to do. First, the phone call to Dak. She went into Isaac's study and closed the door. She wanted privacy for this conversation.

Isaac's study was a masculine lair with a massive oak desk, book shelves on two walls, a worn leather chair and footstool, and various photos and mementos scattered around. Mabel despaired of ever cleaning this room because Isaac didn't want his things disturbed. There were stacks of papers and mail on the desk and small bits of paper with names or phone numbers written on them. Isaac sometimes cleared his clutter a little, usually finding a note or name he thought was lost.

Analee loved to sit in here and just watch her Dad or discuss business or anything else that came up. Now, she sat at the desk and punched the number Dak had given her.

The ringing phone buzzed in Analee's ear as she counted, one – two – three, then four. Dak's voice came on the answering machine. "Hello, I'm not available now. Please leave a message."

Analee was surprised. She had expected Dak to be at home on Sunday, or at least he had said he would be. She left a message asking him to call back that night and hung up.

Her next call was to TWA for her reservation to London. There was space available late Monday, and she booked it, coach this time. Her days of flying first class were over. She would call Nora in the morning. It would be too late to call now.

* * * * *

Analee spent the evening in her room, organizing her clothes and packing. She would need to take a few more things this trip, since she didn't know how long she would stay. Every few minutes, she glanced at the telephone willing it to ring, but it remained silent. Where was Dak? Why didn't he call?

It was nearly ten o'clock when the call finally came. Analee was trembling. "Hello," her voice quavered.

"Hello, Princess." Dak sounded warm and loving. "It was a surprise to get your call. Do you miss me?" he teased.

"Yes, I do, but that's not the reason I called. Do you remember the call I had from Nora in London?"

"Yes, what happened?" Dak sounded anxious.

"Nora's husband, Martin, is very ill and is being transferred to a private hospital in London. Nora has no one. I'm going over for a short time to help her get settled."

"How long will you be away?" Dak's voice had cooled.

"A few weeks, I suppose. It depends on Nora's situation."

"Well, let me know when you get back. I'll probably be moved to Cincinnati by then. We can get together again later."

"Oh, Dak, I'm so sorry this has come up just now. But, Nora is my best friend, and she needs me. Do you understand at all?" Analee pleaded softly.

"Yes, of course. You must go to your friend. I'll be waiting. Send me a post card, and let me know how you're doing."

Analee was uneasy about Dak's tone of voice. He was not the same, somehow.

"Yes, I will write," she said briskly. "Hope to see you when I return."

"Sure thing. Bye, Princess."

"Goodbye, Dak."

Analee replaced the receiver slowly. Something was wrong

here. She would worry until she got back. Not a good way to start a romance.

* * * * *

Monday dawned bright and clear. Analee was awake before dawn. She had spent a restless night, worrying about Dak and their relationship, or lack thereof. Maybe this was another failure – she had had enough of those!

Analee turned on the light, checked the time difference, and tapped out Nora's number on the telephone key pad. Nora answered on the first ring and was overjoyed at Analee's news.

"I'm sorry I can't meet you this time," she lamented. "Will you be OK on your own from Gatwick to Victoria Station?"

"Of course I will. Don't worry. I can take a cab from Victoria Station. See you tomorrow morning."

Analee hung up and went down to the kitchen, where she found her mother making coffee.

"Good morning, dear. Do you want some breakfast?"

"Just some toast and coffee." Analee sat down at the round oak table. Mabel poured coffee into a stoneware mug.

"Did you reach Nora this morning?" Mabel questioned.

"Oh yes, and she's thrilled I'm coming." Analee sipped her coffee thoughtfully. "It's Dak I'm worried about."

"Why? What happened?" Mabel's eyes were concerned.

"He sounded strange on the phone last night. I can't decide if he'll wait for me or not."

Mabel sniffed. "He's a fool if he doesn't, but I think he will be here for you. I saw how he looked at you."

"Maybe, but it won't be the first time I've been dumped. I'd better go shower and dress. Is Dad taking me to the airport?"

"Yes, he's gone to get gas in the car. He'll be ready in plenty of time. Now, you'd better hurry," she smiled.

Analee went quickly upstairs and was closing her suitcase when the telephone shrilled. She waited to see if her mother answered in the kitchen, but it rang again. "Hello," she said briskly.

"Hi yourself," Dak's voice came softly through the line. "Are you ready to go?"

"Dak! It's a surprise to hear from you. I thought you would be on the road today."

"I am, Princess, and if it's OK with you, I can meet you at the airport and see you off. Don't want you to leave without a goodbye kiss."

Analee held her breath as Dak spoke. Her heart was beating fast, and her hand shook.

"Oh, yes, yes! Please be there if you can," she breathed. "My Dad will drop me off about one o'clock in the afternoon. The flight is at three."

"Shall I meet you at the TWA ticket counter?" Dak inquired "at one?"

"That will work," Analee answered.

"Great – see you there, Princess." Dak clicked off, and Analee replaced the phone slowly. Then she grinned, grabbed her bag and ran downstairs, calling to her mother.

"Mom, Mom, guess what? Dak's meeting me at the airport to see me off!"

Mabel ran to her daughter and hugged her. "I knew he'd do something like that. He's smitten with you."

Analee hugged her mother back and smiled at the terminology.

Just then, Isaac entered the back door, calling "Lee, are you ready? It's time to go."

"Yes, Dad, I'm all set." Analee replied cheerfully.

Isaac looked carefully into Analee's eyes. "Dak phoned, didn't he?"

Analee fairly danced as she squealed, "Yes, and he's going to be at the airport. Isn't that great?"

Isaac was pleased to see his daughter so happy. "It sure is, honey. Now, let's get going, so you can see Dak. Is this all your luggage?"

Isaac picked up the bags and headed out to the car. Analee hugged her mother again before joining her Dad in the car.

CHAPTER 12

As they approached the airport, Isaac said thoughtfully, "Lee, how serious are you and Dak at this point?"

Analee looked questioningly at her father. "Why do you ask, Dad? Is there a problem I'm not seeing?"

"Oh, no, I don't think so. It's just that separations sometimes force relationships into situations too quickly. If this is the real thing, it will withstand a separation."

"I know, Dad. We're not rushing anything. I'm just happy that Dak wants to see me today. After the way he sounded last night, I wasn't sure."

They pulled up to the curb, and Isaac opened the trunk to unload Analee's bags. The skycap appeared with a cart.

"Need help, Ma'am?"

"Yes, please take me to the TWA ticket counter to check in. I need to get my ticket there."

Isaac kissed Analee's cheek and said, "Have a good trip, honey. Tell Nora 'hello' and do what you can to help her. Do you have enough money?"

"Yes, Dad. I have money, and I'll let you know how things are when I arrive. Take care of *Henry's* – don't work too hard." Analee gave a quick wave and hurried after the skycap. She joined a line waiting at the ticket counter, and her turn came after a short wait. Ticket and boarding pass in hand, Analee turned from the agent and looked around for Dak. There he was, lounging against a post, watching her with a tiny smile on his lips.

Analee stood still for a moment, then made her way through the milling throng to where Dak waited. "Hi," she breathed. "How long have you been here?"

"Just a few minutes. Thought I'd wait till your business was finished. Didn't want to distract you."

Analee laughed. "Oh, you would have distracted me all right. I haven't touched ground since you called this morning."

"Good!" Dak smiled. "I hoped I would have that effect on you." He took her hands and pulled her close. "Let's go get some coffee."

They sat in the coffee shop in a small booth in the corner. It was as intimate as they could get in a public place. "How long do you think you'll be away?" Dak was holding Analee's hand as they sat side by side. Their faces were inches apart.

"I can't say yet. It depends on Martin's progress and Nora's adjustment to his condition. I'm guessing four to six weeks."

Dak's eyes darkened as he frowned. "That's a long time to be apart, Princess. I will miss you." He leaned over and kissed her lightly.

Analee was touched by his tenderness. She was near tears herself. "Dak, may I ask you something?"

"Yes, of course. You may ask me anything." Dak was surprised and puzzled.

"Last night, when you called, you were different, cool somehow. I was worried that you had lost interest. Was something wrong?"

Dak was thoughtful and looked away for a moment. "I must apologize for my attitude last night. My boss and I had a disagreement that left me very upset, in turmoil. Your call was a surprise and I didn't recover quickly enough. I am sorry."

Analee was pleased to hear his apology, although she felt it was just a little too glib. "It's OK; you're here now." Her lips curved into a smile, but her heart was heavy. Dak was hiding something.

Dak knew he hadn't fooled her. He would have to resolve his problem soon, preferably before Analee returned from London.

* * * * *

"Flight 720 is now ready for boarding." The announcement intruded on the silence between Dak and Analee. She welcomed it and began gathering her things.

"What's your hurry, Princess? There's plenty of time."

"I want to board and find my seat, and make sure I have a pillow and blanket." Analee's tone was impersonal now, as she waited for Dak to slide out of the booth first.

"OK, let's go then." Dak stood and offered his hand to help her. As she took his hand, he felt her cold fingers and frowned. He felt sure now that she had perceived his evasive reply to her question.

They made their way down the concourse to the gate, Dak holding Analee's still cold hand. They didn't speak.

Analee surveyed the other passengers, noting that this was a group similar to the last time with a few more business travelers included. She turned to Dak with a forced smile. "It was good of you to see me off. I'll write if you want me to." She spoke quickly, afraid Dak would object.

"Of course, I want to hear from you, Princess." Dak's voice was deep and warm. "I'll even telephone if you'll give me Nora's number."

Analee looked him in the eyes and saw sincerity and – dare she hope – love?

"I have it here in my bag." She snapped open her purse and pulled out a small notebook. The number was transferred to a clean sheet of paper and ripped out of the notebook. "Here it is, Dak. Remember the time difference if you call."

Dak took the paper and then pulled Analee into his arms. He held her close for several seconds, then pulled back enough to find her mouth. Her response was warm, needy. Dak's lips were soft and tender on hers. The sound coming from his throat was a contented hum. Analee pulled away, flushed and shaking.

"I-I've got to go," she stammered and stepped back, nearly crashing into a man intent on being next in line.

"Sorry, I ---" she began, then gasped. The man was Gus!

"Well, hello again," Gus began, then noticed Dak still holding Analee's hand. "Sorry, I didn't mean to intrude. Talk to you later, Miss Webster." Gus resumed his path to the boarding door.

Analee blushed and looked down, wishing the floor would open and swallow her. Dak noted her discomfort but said nothing.

"Goodbye, Dak." Analee edged away, waving. Dak lifted his

hand. "Have a safe trip, Princess. I'll call you."

Dak watched as Analee disappeared into the crowd. He wondered if the man who had spoken to her was a friend or something more. She had seemed nervous. Dak knew so little about Analee's past. That was something he wanted to change.

First, he needed to clean up his own act. He had not been entirely truthful when Analee questioned him about his attitude on the phone. He had been upset, but it wasn't his boss who did it. Dak had had a brief marriage at age twenty. The girl was twenty-two and had charmed the young man into marriage; then, she changed into what Dak now realized was her true self. She was lazy and sloppy, expecting Dak to wait on her constantly. Dak knew the marriage was a mistake as soon as the honeymoon was over. Jill had insisted on honeymooning in Acapulco, which had taken most of his meager savings. His parents had given him a little money to help out, and Dak wanted to use it as a nest egg. Jill claimed they would never have such a good opportunity to experience Acapulco again. She wheedled Dak into spending the money.

The small apartment they rented was a constant source of complaints by Jill. It was cramped, dark, grimy, and noisy according to her. She constantly nagged at Dak to move, even though his salary barely stretched to cover their current situation. Any suggestion that Jill get a job was met with cold silence or screaming rage. It was her intent to stay home, watch television, and read magazines. Dak was to be the breadwinner and provide for her every whim. As soon as he could swing it, he moved out. His parents took him in until he could sort things out.

Jill continued to harass Dak for what she called "all-my-money", her version of alimony. Dak's father found a competent attorney to help Dak fight Jill's demands, but she was not giving up easily. The divorce was granted with alimony to be paid for two years. Dak thought the settlement excessive; Jill thought it paltry and had her attorney negotiating for more. She occasionally phoned Dak just to remind him of her nagging presence in his life.

This was the call Dak had received just before Analee phoned him on Sunday night. He wanted to explain it all to Analee and would do so as soon as the time was right. Dak walked slowly to his car with thoughts of Analee's sweet innocence mixed in with Jill's grasping greed, knowing it would all need to be resolved soon.

CHAPTER 13

Analee found her assigned seat in the economy section. No first class this trip. Luckily, she had a three-seat section to herself. Gus was nowhere to be seen, and she supposed he was in first class again.

She settled her carryon bag under the seat, selected a blanket and pillow from the overhead bin, and opened a book. Her mind spun as she looked blindly at the words on the page. Gus's appearance after months of silence had unnerved her. She was torn between Gus and Dak. The attraction to Gus was still there, even though Dak seemed to have captured her heart. This was a dilemma she was unfamiliar with. Having two men interested was a new experience.

The flight was underway, and the meal served before Analee was able to relax somewhat. She began to watch the movie, absorbed in the plot, when a figure appeared beside her seat. "May I sit down?" Gus's voice penetrated her concentration.

She blinked twice. "Y-Yes." She moved over to make room.

"I looked for you in first class. What are you doing back here?" Gus was smiling with interest.

"This trip isn't a vacation. I'm going to help my friend Nora, whose husband is ill."

"Martin is ill?" Gus asked with concern. "What happened?"

"He became ill while they were on their honeymoon in Paris. It's a debilitating, incurable disease, and he's being placed in a special facility in London. Nora needs my help to adjust and settle their affairs."

"What a terrible thing to have happen." Gus was sympathetic. "Is there anything I can do?"

"Not that I know of now, but it's nice of you to ask."

Gus watched Analee for a moment, noting her fingers twisting together nervously. "You must be very worried about Nora," Gus began, then stopped as Analee looked up at him with pain-filled eyes. He was puzzled. Her expression was more than just worry for Nora. "My dear, what's wrong?" he said, turning to take her hands.

Analee could not speak. How was she to explain her feeling of rejection when he had broken his promise to contact her all those months ago? Pulling herself together, she forced a smile. "You're right; I am worried about Nora. Sometimes it's overwhelming. Now, tell me your reason for traveling today."

Gus thought she was covering up a deeper reason, but he didn't probe. Instead, he told her, "I'm returning to London to finish with Elspeth's job. It's a matter of inspection, actually. The computers are all installed. I just need to do a final check."

Elspeth was the reason Gus had left her nearly stranded in London, Analee thought. So, she was still pulling Gus' strings; only he didn't know it.

"How is Elspeth?" Analee asked dully, not really caring.

"Oh, she's up to her old tricks" Gus grinned. " She insisted I make this trip, and when I balked, she sent a ticket. I got her number last time. She won't make a fool of me again."

Analee wasn't convinced but was cheered by Gus's words.

"Is Nora meeting you at Gatwick?" Gus questioned.

"No, I'm taking the train to Victoria Station, then a cab from there."

"Then, you can share the car Elspeth is sending for me. We can drop you off at Victoria." With that, Gus stood and smiled at Analee. "I'll let you relax and watch the movie. Better sleep a little, if you can. See you when we land."

Analee laid her head back and closed her eyes. Gus was so nice. Was it just polite courtesy, or did he really like her? The old shyness came creeping back.

Finding the movie too far gone to catch up with, Analee removed her headset and settled down to sleep for a while. All the events of the day had left her exhausted.

* * * * *

The crowd of passengers surging to the passport check points buffeted Analee, and she struggled to keep her place in line. Everyone was groggy and grumpy so early in the morning. The agents at the check points were unfailingly cheerful as they processed each person, wishing them a "Good Day."

Analee's turn soon came, and she was finally cleared through to "Baggage Reclaim." Once there, she looked for her bag on the carousel. Others were waiting with carts to load up with their luggage. Her bag appeared, and she hoisted it to the floor, wondering how she would manage everything.

Just then, a hand reached down and lifted her bag onto a cart. Gus stood smiling, his crew cut slightly mashed down on one side, evidence of his sleeping position on the plane. His clothes were not rumpled. Analee wondered how he could look so good. She herself felt gritty and unkempt.

"Are you ready to go? The car will be waiting."

Analee nodded, too weary to speak. She followed Gus through the exit doors and past the throng holding signs with names of those to be met. Gus walked rapidly, causing Analee to jog behind him to keep up.

They reached the outer door, and Gus spotted the driver holding a sign with "HERMAN – CORPORATE SUITES" printed on it. "Here we are. Get in, and I'll take care of the bags." Analee sank into the plush seat and closed her eyes. What a treat to have a ride into London. She didn't think she could have managed the train after all.

A cool voice caused her eyes to fly open.

"I see Gus is taking in strays again." Elspeth Sheffield sat in the opposite seat of the limousine, looking as if she had spent the last hours in a salon. Her hair was perfect, designer clothes enhancing her figure, and long legs demurely crossed at the ankles.

"Do I know you? You do look familiar." Elspeth leaned forward for a better look. "Oh yes, you're that little American friend of Nora's. What are you doing here this time?"

Before Analee could reply, Gus stepped into the car and pulled the door closed. He immediately felt the tension and his eyes roved the interior of the vehicle.

Elspeth fixed her gaze on Gus and waited for him to speak.

"Hello Elspeth. You didn't need to meet me so early. Our business can wait until after breakfast."

Elspeth smiled and reached a hand to Gus. "I couldn't wait to see you again, darling" she breathed. "But why is she here?" Elspeth nodded to Analee as she spoke.

"*Analee* needed a ride to Victoria Station" Gus emphasized her name to Elspeth. "I knew it was on the way to Corporate Suites, so I offered to drop her off."

"You are a gentleman," Elspeth purred, thinking to herself that he was a fool to take an interest in such a plain, mousy girl, when she Elspeth was so much better.

Analee felt uncomfortable under Elspeth's cool scrutiny, shrinking back into the corner of the seat as far as she could. Gus noted the exchange, but said nothing. The limousine rolled along the motorway toward London.

Analee dozed as Gus and Elspeth quietly began discussing business. When the car stopped, she jerked awake, confused by her surroundings. "Where are we?" she squeaked.

"At Victoria Station," Gus answered, patting her arm. "You can get a cab here. The driver has your bag set out. I'll see you on your way."

They slid out of the limousine while Elspeth watched, a smug smile on her lips. She flapped her hand as a farewell to Analee but said nothing.

Gus signaled to a cab and helped Analee inside. "I'll call you at Nora's as soon as I can. Give Nora my regards, and take care." He closed the door and stepped back, as the cab drew away into the stream of traffic.

Analee drew a deep breath as she focused on the bustle of London around her. The rush and energy intrigued her as it had on her first visit. There was something about the city that drew her interest.

CHAPTER 14

Arriving at Nora's little house was like coming home. The driver stopped in the narrow street and helped Analee unload her bags. She paid him, adding a generous tip.

"Thank ye, Ma'am," he grinned. "'Ave a good visit wit' yer friend." He climbed back into the driver's seat and rumbled off.

Analee turned to look at Nora's front door. It flew open, and Nora came running.

"Oh Lee, I'm so glad you're here. Let's get your things inside."

The two of them picked up the bags and went into the house. Even though her previous stay had been short, Analee felt welcomed and warmed by the charming little house. She took a deep breath and turned to Nora. They hugged, and Analee saw tears in Nora's eyes.

"I'm so sorry about Martin. How is he?"

Nora's voice was choked. "Not good, I'm afraid. The trip back from Paris was almost more than he could take. He's very weak. We can go see him this afternoon."

Analee took charge saying, "Let's have some tea and biscuits; then I'll unpack." They both smiled, remembering Analee's puzzlement at the word "biscuit" on her first visit.

As they drank tea, Nora filled her in on the details of Martin's illness. To change the subject, Analee told Nora about Dak and about meeting Gus again on the plane.

"Will you see Gus while you're here?" Nora questioned.

"I don't know. He may not call. After all, Elspeth has her hooks in deep."

"Oh, Elspeth," Nora snorted. "She likes the chase, but the catch is not her style. Gus can shed her like a fur coat in July."

"We'll see, won't we?" Analee replied, somewhat cheered by Nora's words.

They finished their tea, and Analee went to unpack and freshen up. Nora was waiting, keys jangling, as Analee stepped out of the little bedroom.

"It's time to be off. Martin will be anxious to see us."

Nora drove swiftly through the busy streets. They arrived at the private hospital in less than thirty minutes. The sign in front read simply "*The Winchester,*" and the structure appeared to be a large private residence. The two women entered through a side door which led to a small foyer. A reception desk was situated in a corner, surrounded by large potted plants. A small woman sat behind the desk. Analee thought she looked like a bird perched in the trees.

The voice that greeted them was not bird-like; rather, it was more like soft music. "Hello, Nora my dear," the music continued. "This must be Analee." The woman reached out and took Analee's hand. "Welcome to *The Winchester.* I'm Julia Holborn, Director. Nora has spoken highly of you."

Analee felt a warm current from Julia's hand. Martin was surely in good hands. "I'm happy to meet you, Ms. Holborn."

Analee turned to Nora. "Do you want to see Martin alone?"

"No, you come along. He wants to see both of us."

Nora led the way up the curving stairway to the first floor, explaining to Analee, that in England it is customary to name the first floor "ground" and then first, second, etc.

Analee thought again how the building was more like a small hotel, or private home.

Nora continued along the spacious hallway, stopping at the last doorway. The door stood slightly ajar, and voices could be heard coming from the room.

"Just one more bite, Martin. You can do it. There now, your sweet Nora will be here soon." The soft tinkle of a spoon against a dish was followed by the swish of shoes on carpet. The door opened, and a uniformed nurse proceeded past them. She smiled at Nora and jerked her head back toward the room.

"He's waiting for you, Mrs. Giles. Doing quite well today."

Nora and Analee stepped softly into the room. It was a large corner room furnished with comfortable wingback chairs and polished wood tables. If it had not been for the hospital bed upon which Martin lay, the room could have been taken for a master bedroom or hotel suite. The colors were a soft blue with mauve accents, the carpeting a deep rose.

One look at Martin caused Analee to gasp. She covered her mouth as if to cough, hoping her shocked eyes wouldn't give her away. Martin was so thin she could almost see his bones. His skin was pale and his veins stood out like lines drawn in ink. Just then, he smiled at Analee, and for a fleeting instant the old Martin appeared. She remembered his smile and how charmed she had been by it.

"Hi Lee," Martin whispered. "Good of you to come."

Nora leaned over to kiss him. "Don't talk, darling. Lee's here now to help me. You needn't worry about a thing." She held Martin's hand, and they looked into each other's eyes.

Analee felt the love gleaming between them with sorrow mixed in. She stepped back, but Nora motioned her closer.

"Tell Martin about your trip and about meeting Gus again."

Analee began her story, making it cheerful and funny, succeeding in bringing several quick smiles to Martin's face.

"Gus is a good man," he whispered. "Don't let him get away."

The door opened, and the same nurse entered the room, carrying a tray. "Time for your medication, Martin." Her voice was soft and melodious.

Martin grimaced but swallowed the small cup of liquid she handed him, holding his head up to help. She then prepared an injection, which she gave in his hip. She reached skillfully under the sheet, so that his modesty was not disturbed. "There now, that should help you through the next few hours." She smiled, turned, and swished out of the room.

Nora returned to her chair by the bed and picked up Martin's hand. "We'll go now, dear, and let you rest. I'll be back later to tuck you in." She leaned over and kissed him.

Analee touched his hand lightly and murmured her goodbye. The two left the room and went back downstairs without speaking.

Nora had tears in her eyes when she turned to Analee. "It is so hard to see him like this. I'm all torn up inside."

Analee reached out and gathered Nora in her arms. No words came, but she knew Nora could feel her empathy.

They walked arm in arm to the car. Nora drove a while before she spoke. "Let's go have an early dinner; then, I'll drop you at home before I go back to *The Winchester.* Martin likes me to be there when he goes to sleep."

"Are you sure? I can stay with you if you need me."

"No, Lee, you need to get over jet lag. You're starting to droop already."

Nora drove to a small Italian restaurant not far from her home. The owner greeted them at the door, taking Nora's hands and kissing them.

"Ah, Miss Nora, and how are you tonight?"

"Very well, Tony," Nora replied, turning to Analee. "This is my dear friend Analee Webster from America. She has come to stay with me until I can sort things out."

Tony took Analee's hands and smiled. "Miss Webster, it is a pleasure. You are very good to help Miss Nora. Come, come, sit down. I will bring you some wine."

The women sat where Tony directed them. Soon, wine and huge plates of food were set before them. Analee laughed and asked, "Do they always know what you want to eat, or do you eat whatever they bring?"

Nora patted her mouth with the checkered napkin. "Tony's food is all delicious, so I don't care what he serves. Martin and I used to come here all the time." Her voice choked off, and she covered her face with the napkin. "Oh, Lee, I don't think I can go on without Martin. He's dying, you know."

Nora's quiet sobs made Analee turn from her own dinner to comfort her friend. She touched Nora's arm gently. "I'm so sorry. I'm here for you. Whatever it takes, we'll get through this together."

"I know. I'm grateful you were able to come, but it's so *hard!"* Nora's voice broke again, and she leaned her head on her arms.

Tony bustled over, noting Nora's distress. "Miss Nora, is there anything I can do? Please don't cry." He gave a little laugh. "It upsets my customers."

Nora raised her head. With a watery smile she said, "Thanks, Tony. I think we'll be leaving now. I just had a small panic attack."

As they gathered their things, Tony waved away their attempt to pay him, saying it was his way of helping Martin.

Nora drove slowly without speaking. Analee worried that Nora was ill. "Are you sure you should go back to *The Winchester* tonight? Maybe you need to go home and rest."

Nora smiled wanly. "Thanks, Lee, but Martin expects me. I'll be all right."

They reached Nora's house, and Analee got out. Nora waited until she was inside the front door, then roared off.

CHAPTER 15

It was nearly eleven o'clock before Nora returned. Analee was worried. She was curled up on the sofa, trying to read a book, without much success. The small noises in the quiet house were distracting and unfamiliar. A tree branch scraping on a window had nearly sent her into a panic, and the refrigerator's hum sounded like an engine to her frightened ears.

A new clicking had her clutching a sofa cushion in terror until she realized it was Nora's key in the front door. She saw Nora's tired eyes and was ashamed she had been such a mouse.

Nora sat down and patted Analee's hand. "He's sleeping at last. He had another attack this evening, and it took longer to calm him." Analee gathered Nora into her arms, and they rocked together silently.

"Let's go to bed. Things always seem worse in the dark of night." Analee felt Nora's shoulders droop as she spoke.

"OK. I am tired, but I doubt that I can sleep."

"Well, just rest then. It will do you good to lie down." Analee helped Nora to her feet. "Do you want me to get you a glass of milk?"

"No, thanks Lee. You go on to bed. I'll see you in the morning. Sleep as late as you want. We don't have to get up early."

"All right, then. Good night, Nora."

Analee closed the door to her little bedroom and climbed into bed. She drifted to sleep as the tree outside scratched a soft rhythm on the window.

Morning brought sunshine and warm breezes to Analee's senses. The smell of brewing coffee wafted past her nose. Her eyes opened slowly. The window was open, and the air smelled fresh. Nora's head appeared in the doorway. "Hey sleepyhead, are you awake yet? It's nearly nine o'clock."

Analee scrambled out of bed and thrust her arms into a robe. "Be right there," she called.

The kitchen was fragrant with coffee and baking rolls. Nora lifted a pan from the oven as Analee watched from the doorway.

"You are certainly cheerful this morning, Nora. Did you sleep after all?"

"I did that." Nora smiled. "And things do seem better in the daylight. What a wise one you are!"

"I was just quoting my dad." Analee laughed. "He's always saying that."

Nora nodded her agreement and motioned Analee to sit down. She poured coffee for both of them. The pan of rolls was placed on the table between them. "I'm sorry about last night," Nora began. "Sometimes, I'm overwhelmed with all of it."

"No need to apologize, Nora. Now, what can I do today?"

"There are two applicants for housekeeper coming by. I want you to interview them, and choose one to hire. The first is at eleven o'clock and the other at one o'clock. If neither seems right, call the agency, and ask for more applicants. Here's the number."

Nora hurried off to dress. Analee finished her coffee and cleared the table. She was about to leave the kitchen when Nora appeared, purse in hand.

"I'm off to *The Winchester.* If I don't get back before lunch time, help yourself to whatever you want to eat. The pantry is stocked." Waving, Nora breezed out the door, leaving Analee gaping after her.

"Well then," Analee thought, "I'd better get dressed and ready for the first interview."

Promptly at eleven, the doorbell chimed. Analee opened the door and suppressed a giggle. The woman standing there could have been Mary Poppins herself. The resemblance was startling.

"Good morning. I am Helen Perkins, here to interview for a position as housekeeper."

Analee held the door wider for the woman and said, "Come in. You're very prompt." Still chuckling to herself, Analee led Mrs. Perkins to the living room and directed her to a chair.

The woman handed a sheaf of papers to Analee. "Here are my references." She spoke precisely. "My last position was with the Maestro and his family. They moved to Vienna." She looked sad. Analee wondered if Mrs. Perkins had wanted to go with them.

After a few questions and conversation, Analee decided she liked the woman, but thought she might be a little too stiff for Nora. Analee showed Mrs. Perkins out with the assurance they would let her have a decision soon.

Just then, the telephone rang. Analee answered tentatively. "Hello, Giles residence."

"Analee, is that you?" The voice was warm and familiar. "This is Gus."

Analee drew in her breath sharply. "Hello Gus. How are you?"

"Fine, fine. I'm finishing with Elspeth today and hoped you might be free for dinner tonight."

"I-I'll have to see what Nora's plans are. She's with Martin now."

"I'm at the Park Lane Hotel. Call me as soon as you can. The dining room here is excellent. I have reservations for 7:00 p.m." His voice lowered and softened. "I really want to see you, Lee."

Analee shivered as though a strange warning was surging through her blood. "Thank you, Gus." She nearly whispered. "I will call as soon as I can. Goodbye."

She stood, holding the phone, dreaming of what Gus had said. "He wants to see me, ME!" she thought. "After Elspeth, what could he see in me?"

Analee was finishing her sandwich when Nora came in. "Oh, good. You found food. I'll just grab a snack; then, we can interview the one o'clock together." They discussed Helen Perkins, Nora laughing at Analee's description of "Mary Poppins." "If this one isn't right, we'll call the agency."

Josephine Post proved to be exactly right. She was short and round, with a hearty laugh, and eyes that nearly closed when she smiled which was most of the time. Her dark hair was pulled into a neat topknot. She wore a simple black dress and carried a large tote bag. As she sat with Nora and Analee, she dug into her bag and pulled out a large, pink apron.

"I can start right now if you need me," she said, standing and tying the apron over her roundness. "You two appear to be floundering."

Nora and Analee looked at each other, grinning. Nora shrugged. "Your references are good. If the salary is adequate, you're hired."

Josephine nodded in satisfaction. "Yes, indeed it is. Now, where is the kitchen?"

Josephine settled in, mothering the two younger women, cooking and cleaning with a happy attitude that made Nora's little house glow.

When Analee asked Nora if she should go to dinner with Gus, Nora quickly said, "Yes. Go and have fun, I'll be with Martin all evening, anyway."

* * * * *

Gus was waiting in the lounge at the Park Lane Hotel as Analee stepped in. A young man played romantic tunes on the grand piano. Settees and small chairs were occupied by chatting groups of tourists and locals alike, all choosing the genteel atmosphere over a traditional pub.

Gus rose to greet Analee and took her hand as they sat together in front of a small fireplace. "First, let me apologize for not calling you back home. My business has kept me on the run constantly. If I had a free minute, it was too late at night to call."

Analee watched his eyes as he talked, thinking they were so deep she could nearly drown in them. The honesty shone like beacons to her heart. Gus still held her hand. She squeezed his gently. "It's OK. I did wonder what happened to you, but I've been busy, too." All her previous insecurities faded away in the depths of Gus's eyes.

Gus was pleased to see her reaction. It fit into his plans for their future together.

"Tell me what you've been doing since we last saw each other?" Gus questioned.

Analee described *Henry's* to him, with her plan to take over full management in time.

Gus was intrigued with this woman. She was so shy, yet intelligent. When she spoke of her father, the love and respect glowed on her face. He had a high regard for anyone with family ties as close as hers. But, Gus had a dark side that Analee had not yet discovered.

The conversation continued through dinner. For Analee, the time fairly flew. Gus listened attentively, asking questions to keep her talking about herself. He guessed that didn't happen often. He suggested an after dinner drink at *The Dorchester*, describing the luxury hotel so eloquently that Analee could not refuse.

The cab drew up to the portico of *The Dorchester*, and a doorman sprang to open the door. Gus and Analee alighted on a red carpet that led to the large, brass-framed double doors, being held open by another uniformed doorman. Analee held Gus's arm as they entered. She was a little uneasy here; everything was so elegant.

They found a corner table in the bar and ordered drinks. Gus slid across the bench to be near Analee and reached for her hand. "You are a charming woman, Lee. May I see you again before I go back to the States?"

"Yes, if Nora can spare me another evening."

"I was thinking about tomorrow, being together all day. We could tour the Canterbury Cathedral. Have you ever been there?"

Analee drew in a long breath. "I'm not sure I should leave Nora all day, although we did hire a housekeeper today. Her name is Josephine."

Gus smiled. "Josephine, huh? Sounds very competent to me. Surely she can take care of Nora."

Analee smiled while gazing around the ornate room, observing the other patrons. They all seemed to be deeply engrossed in conversation, huddled over drinks. One table of four women captured her attention. Two of the women appeared to be American, laughing softly as one of the others leaned over as if telling a joke. All were dressed in evening gowns, apparently having attended a formal function of some kind.

"They look so self-assured, confident." Analee thought to herself, "I must appear to be a drudge next to them."

Gus followed her gaze and saw the uncertainty on her face. "Would you like to meet them?" he asked. "One of the women works for Elspeth at Corporate Suites."

"Oh, no thanks." Analee blushed and ducked her head. "They have their own little group and wouldn't be interested in me."

"Well then, are you ready to go?" Gus stood and held out his hand to Analee.

Analee felt foolish and awkward until they were in a cab on their way to Nora's. Gus was silent as they drove through the London streets. Analee was certain he would forget about the invitation for the next day. The cab stopped in front of Nora's house. Gus helped Analee out, instructing the driver to wait.

At the door Analee turned to say "goodnight" and found Gus reaching to kiss her. His arms folded around her shoulders. He lowered his head to meet her lips. Analee shivered as she had when Gus phoned. His kiss was warm and sweet. Hugging her lightly, Gus said, "I'll call early tomorrow to see if you can get away. Good night, dear Lee." He loped down the steps to the cab, waving as he closed the door. Analee stood, rooted to the spot. Confusion ran rampant through her mind. Gus really did want to see her again! But she had been such a bore, she thought.

Quietly, she opened the door, expecting Nora to be sleeping. Instead, she found Nora lounging on the couch, a Mozart piano concerto playing on the stereo.

"Music always relaxes me," Nora said in response to Analee's questioning look. "Especially Mozart. It's so structured. Puts my mind back in order." She stood up. "Did you have a good time? How long is Gus staying in London? Will you see him again?"

The questions flew at Analee as Nora began pacing the room.

"Nora, please sit down. You must be exhausted. I didn't expect you to wait up for me."

"OK, but tell me all about your date." Nora perched on the edge of the couch and clasped her hands around her knees.

Analee described the Park Lane and the dinner, then drinks at *The Dorchester.*

"Wow, he must be on an expense account!" Nora exclaimed. "That wasn't a cheap evening."

"He wants me to go to Canterbury with him tomorrow. I don't

think I should go and desert you. This isn't a vacation – I'm here to help you." Analee paced as Nora had done, causing Nora to stifle a smile.

"I can spare you for one day. Anyway, with Josephine coming, there isn't much for you to do here. I think you should go."

Analee stopped pacing, looking at Nora in surprise. "Are you sure? I didn't give him a definite answer."

Nora rose and hugged Analee. "Let's get some sleep, so you'll be ready for your big day tomorrow."

CHAPTER 16

The day dawned bright and clear, which gave Analee hope that it was a good omen. True to his word, Gus telephoned at 9:00 a.m., saying he would pick her up in an hour.

Nora was dressed and ready to leave for *The Winchester* when Gus arrived. She answered the door. "Hello Gus. You're looking well," she greeted.

Gus shook Nora's hand. "How is Martin? I'm so sorry to hear he is ill."

"He's dying by inches." Nora's voice was sad. "But I have made him as comfortable as possible, and he's getting good care. It's all I can do."

Gus nodded sympathetically.

Analee entered the living room, noting Gus's casual attire. He looked so handsome in his open collar shirt and khakis. A dark blue blazer hung over his arm.

"Good morning, Lee," he grinned. "All set?"

"Umm yes, I'll get my bag."

"Bye bye. Have a good time. No need to hurry back." Nora waved them out the door.

Gus had hired a car, and they drove swiftly through the streets and roundabouts until they were in open country. Analee relaxed a little, happily looking at the passing scenes.

Gus turned his head, smiling at her, pleased that she was enjoying herself. They came to a small park near the cathedral. Gus pulled off the road, stopping in a shady spot. "Are you hungry?" he asked. "I brought a hamper."

Analee watched, fascinated, as Gus pulled an enormous basket out of the boot. Grinning, she asked, "Did you stay up all night preparing this?"

Gus answered with a grin of his own. "My secret."

They spread a blanket on the soft grass and opened the hamper. Analee's eyes widened when she saw the contents. Goodies of every description were packed into its interior, even a bottle of wine and crystal goblets. Gus spread it all out and opened the wine. "To us," he toasted, and they both sipped.

After they had sampled the food and drunk most of the wine, Gus lay on his back, hands stacked beneath his head. Analee sat watching him aware of his male form, attracted in spite of herself.

Gus glanced lazily at her. "Join me?" he asked softly.

Hiding an uneasy feeling, Analee moved closer on the blanket but sat primly, legs tucked under her.

"Oh, come on. Lie down here with me. I want to feel your body next to mine." Gus reached out and pulled Analee's arm.

She wrenched her arm away and scrambled to her feet. "I-I don't think that's a good idea," she stammered. Blushing, she folded her arms and turned away. Gus was different today. She didn't like it very much.

Gus stood behind her, touching her shoulders. "I'm sorry, Lee. I'm rushing you, but we both know where this is headed."

Analee was uncomfortable now. She had to tell him soon. Turning to face him, she saw in his eyes that he was serious. How would he react when he knew about her intent to wait for a serious commitment?

Before Analee could speak, Gus began gathering their things and repacking the basket. "We'd better go see the cathedral. The tours are stopped while they have services."

Analee settled herself in the car while Gus closed the boot and started the car. They drove to the parking area near the magnificent Canterbury Cathedral. "This is the Mother Church, you know. Thomas Becket was murdered here," Gus informed her somberly.

Analee admired the old building, inspired by its beauty and charm. They entered the huge doors and heard organ music from somewhere above them. Analee forgot her doubts and fears, swept away by the history surrounding her. The afternoon slipped away and it was soon time to leave. Gus had been attentive and informative, reading from his guidebook as they viewed the ancient sites.

Now on the road back to London, Gus once again broached the subject of their relationship. "Analee, I want to take our relationship to the next level," he said in a soft, sweet voice. "How do you feel about that?"

Analee was shocked into silence. She was confused. Did the "next level" mean being intimate? Or, did every man think that was inevitable in a relationship? She was so quiet, Gus thought she hadn't heard him, but then, she turned to him with tears of fright in her eyes.

"I can't, Gus. If I have given you the wrong impression, I'm sorry." She saw his mouth tighten, and his eyes go cold.

"You certainly did give me the wrong impression," Gus almost growled. "You were sending out definite signals that you were interested in me."

Analee was confused even more. What signals was he talking about? She was not aware of any and didn't even know *how!* Gus's attitude was a mystery.

"We are near the car hire lot where I must return the car. You can get a cab to Nora's." Gus's voice was hard as steel.

Analee was miserable, shrinking in the corner of the seat. No need to aggravate Gus any further.

They reached the car park. Gus stopped and yanked open her door. "Go!" he snarled. "Here's cab fare." He thrust some bills in her hand. He turned and strode away, leaving Analee standing, bewildered and hurt.

Thankfully, Nora was out when Analee arrived, so she didn't have to explain anything yet. Her thoughts were jumbled and confused. Gus had hurt her deeply, but at the same time, she was angry at him for expecting her to be 'easy.' "Not many women have such scruples these days," Analee mused. Still, she had enjoyed his company and had thought he was a sincere friend. "Wrong again," she thought. "Will I ever learn about men?"

By the time Nora arrived, Analee had calmed herself and was able to describe her day with Gus without showing her hurt and anger.

"Lee, there's more to this than you are telling. What happened? Are you seeing him again?" Nora demanded.

Analee sighed. "You can always read me so well, Nora. Gus wanted more than I was willing to give, and I said 'no'. He was angry and stormed off. I took a cab from the car hire."

"That's it? Gus was only interested in sex? I'm very disappointed in him for that. I gave him more credit. Well, you're better off without him," Nora declared. "Let's have a glass of wine and see what Josephine has left us for dinner."

They had a quiet meal and went to bed early, both women exhausted from emotional turmoil.

CHAPTER 17

Analee was awakened by a knock on her door. She struggled to find her voice to call out "come in."

Nora stepped into the room, holding a handkerchief to her tear-filled eyes. "Oh, Lee, Martin's gone. The hospital just rang to tell me. He died suddenly about an hour ago."

Nora sat on Lee's bed, sobbing. Analee put her arms around her friend and held her close, her own eyes filling with tears. "How sad for you that you weren't with him. But, it's good that he didn't suffer or have much pain."

Nora's voice was muffled. "I know, but it's so hard to let him go."

Analee held Nora gently, letting her cry it out. After a few minutes Nora took a deep breath and patted Analee's hand. "There are arrangements to make and people to phone. I had better get started."

"I'll help you. Just give me a few minutes to get dressed." Analee hurried to the bathroom as she spoke.

* * * * *

Later that day, the two women were finished with all the arrangements and were sitting in Nora's living room. Josephine had just brought them tea.

"This is just what we needed," Analee said. "Good, strong English tea."

"You've become very British in a short time, Lee," Nora smiled. " I don't know how I managed before you came."

Analee sipped her tea and heard Josephine answer the telephone. In a moment Josephine appeared in the doorway. "Call for you, Miss Analee. It's from the States."

Analee hurried to pick up the phone. "Hello," she breathed.

"Hi Princess, how's it going?" Dak's voice boomed through the receiver.

"Dak! I'm so glad to hear your voice. I miss you." Analee stopped, choked on tears.

"Honey, what's wrong? Has something happened?" Concern flooded Dak's voice.

"Martin died last night. We're coping but not very well."

"I'm so sorry to hear this. Please tell Nora she has my deepest sympathy. Will you be coming home soon?"

"I don't know yet. I can't leave Nora until I'm sure she will be all right."

"Just hurry as soon as you can. I'll call again in a couple of days. Lee, I-I miss you." Dak's voice was soft and warm as he hung up.

Analee walked slowly back to Nora, suddenly feeling homesick. Hearing Dak's voice had given her an unexpected thrill. Could it be that she was falling in love with Dak? After the disaster with Gus, she wanted to be very sure of Dak and their feelings for each other.

* * * * *

Martin's funeral brought many friends to pay their respects. Nora greeted each one with affection, while Analee watched her for signs of fatigue. Nora was running on nerves. Analee wanted to prevent a breakdown if she could.

It was finally over. After they had closed the door on the last group of mourners, both women collapsed on the couch and kicked off their shoes.

"I'm so tired. Hope I can sleep tonight," Nora sighed. "Is it awful for me to feel relieved?"

"I don't think so, Nora," Analee said thoughtfully. "You've been under a big strain for a long time, and now it's over. You'll grieve, of course, but relief is a natural feeling."

"You always know the right thing to say. I'll be sorry to see you leave."

Josephine entered the room quietly, waiting until the conversation stopped. "Will you be wanting dinner, Miss Nora? I have soup already made, and there's fresh bread."

"That sounds lovely, Josephine. We'll be right in."

Nora and Analee stood, linking arms as they walked into the dining room. "I'm so lucky to have found Josephine!" Nora exclaimed. "She's a treasure."

* * * * *

In the days that followed, Nora seemed to be picking up the pieces, putting her life back together. She spoke with friends from the music academy who urged her to return to studying and performing.

Analee quietly made plans to return home. Dak continued to telephone every few days, making her anxious to see him again.

One evening after dinner, Nora and Analee sat listening to Mozart; both women silently restructuring their lives.

Nora spoke first. "Lee, it's time you went home. I have loved having you here, and God knows I needed you, especially the last few weeks. But, you need to get on with your life, too."

Analee smiled. "How did you know I was just about to say that very same thing? You're right, of course. My flight is booked for the day after tomorrow. Dak has promised to meet me."

"Good for you. I think you have found the right man. Now, let's go to bed. We have a lot to do tomorrow." Nora stood yawning, both heading for their bedrooms.

* * * * *

The next day Nora and Analee stood near the barrier beyond which only ticketed passengers could go.

"Goodbye, my friend. You're almost a sister. I love you for all you have given me." Nora hugged Analee close as tears rolled down her cheeks.

"I love you too, Nora. Please don't cry, or I'll blubber all the way home. Dak won't want me red-eyed." Analee tried to joke.

Nora drew back and smiled through her tears. "Have a good trip. Write lots of letters. I want full reports on your romance."

Analee waved as she moved down the line, through security, and out of Nora's sight.

* * * * *

Dak waited and watched for the plane. The board showed "on time," but so far there was no sign of the plane bringing Analee home to him. Her absence had given him time to think. He realized she was his kind of woman. He only hoped she had similar feelings for him. And, he wanted to know how Gus figured into the picture.

The crowd at the gate stirred, moving toward the door as the airline agent opened it. In a few minutes passengers began deplaning, greeting waiting family and friends as they entered the terminal. Dak strained to see each one, watching for Analee. "There she is!" He spotted her and pushed through the crowd to her side.

"Hi Princess," he said softly, reaching out to take her in his arms.

"Dak." Analee stood still and looked into his eyes. After a long moment she reached for him, too. The embrace was strong, passionate and thrilling. Both of them felt the undercurrent of unspoken emotion.

Clasping her hand in his, Dak laughingly pulled her along. "Let's find your bags and get out of here."

Analee was happy to be home. Seeing Dak, she was more and more certain he was the "right man" as Nora had said. Dak held her hand in the car, telling her all about his business and what he had been doing while she was away. Analee described to him some of the sightseeing she had been able to do on this trip.

Passing a shopping center, Dak pulled into the parking lot. He stopped the car and turned to Analee. "Before we get too far, will you tell me about the man on the plane?"

Analee looked embarrassed. "He was a mistake. Just another broken promise in my life. I seem to attract the wrong kind of man."

"Does that mean I might be wrong, too?"

"I don't think so. You are different, a genuine person. Somehow,

Gus got the wrong idea about me, but I believe you know who I really am. Gus wanted something I couldn't give him. You won't do that, will you?"

Dak shook his head but knew he had to tell her about his previous marriage. He decided there was no better time than now. He began by taking Analee's hand and started to tell the unhappy story.

Analee looked at Dak with sad eyes, once again wondering about her choice of men. She sat for a minute, thinking about the difference between Dak and Gus. Dak watched her, knowing what was going through her mind, but waited for her to speak.

Finally, Analee said "Dak, I don't care what happened in the past. I think it has made you a better man. Let's go home."

When they arrived at Analee's home, Mabel and Isaac rushed out to greet them. "Honey, it's good to have you back. Is Nora doing OK? Poor girl, losing her husband so soon." Mabel gushed the words while hugging her daughter.

Isaac waited his turn and grabbed Analee in a bear hug. "Are you really OK, Lee? It has been quite a responsibility for you."

Analee grinned at them all. "I'm fine, now that I'm home. Just let me freshen up before I tell you all about it."

Dak joined Mabel and Isaac in the living room while Analee went upstairs. When she came down, she was struck by the easy familiarity between Dak and her parents.

"Dak has spent quite a lot of time here," Isaac said, noticing his daughter's questioning look.

"They have treated me like a son," Dak said sheepishly, hoping Analee would not be offended.

Mabel rose and started for the kitchen. "I'll make some coffee. There are chocolate chip cookies, Dak's favorite."

Analee looked confused, trying to understand. It seemed as if Dak had made a place for himself with her family. Isaac excused himself, too, leaving Dak and Analee alone.

Taking her hand, Dak led her to the couch and sat beside her. "Lee, I love you. I'm asking you to be my wife. I know this is too fast, and you need time, but I'll wait. I just needed to tell you now."

Analee sat, stunned, thinking of the words she had just heard. "He loves me! I've never heard those words from a man before.

What a sweet sound." Her smile grew, and her eyes sparkled.

"Dak, you're wonderful. I do need a little time, but the outcome looks hopeful."

Then, Mabel and Isaac came into the room together, clapping their hands. "I knew our girl would see that Dak is the one for her," Isaac declared. Mabel nodded agreement.

Dak pulled Analee up and into his arms. Their kiss was the seal of approval, their promise of love.

Epilogue

Dak and Analee were married in less than a year. Analee continued her "on the job training" at *Henry's,* with Isaac gradually bowing out of the business.

After the wedding Isaac told Analee, "We don't need that big house. Our grandchildren can fill it up." He and Mabel moved to a new condo nearby and gave the property to Analee and Dak.

Dak wanted to get off the road, and he did by convincing Restaurant Supply to open an outlet in Bloomington. He became the manager.

Analee and Dak felt blessed to have each other and their "dream home." Their lives had definitely settled into a comfortable, middle-class, Midwest routine. And, they loved it!

* * * * * *

Anowledgements

Thanks to local author Donna Cronk for her encouragement to finish my novel. Retired English teacher Jane Cronk willingly edited my writing with thoughtful and helpful suggestions. Mark Herbkersman has been a guiding force and tremendous help with the publishing process. I am grateful to Joy Herbkersman for her cover design and expertise.

About the Author

Ruth Ann Willis has written several short stories and essays. After retiring from TWA, she decided to write about some of her experiences gathered on trips to London, with various fictional incidents added. This grew into *Broken Promises*. This is her first novel. She would be happy to hear from readers via email – *ruthannsbook@gmail.com*.

64605011R00055

Made in the USA
Middletown, DE
31 August 2019